SHATTERED

SOUL

C.L. Stewart

SHATTERED SOUL

First published 2016
Second edition 2018

www.clstewart.co.uk

ISBN: 978-1-9993193-0-4

For Liz

Your enthusiasm made this possible

ACKNOWLEDGMENTS

First of all I have to thank my dear friend Liz. I remember very well being so embarrassed sending you my first three chapters to read and thinking, *'what have I done?'* When you sent me a message saying you needed to read the rest I was over the moon. I don't think I have ever written so fast and could barely keep up with you. You made me believe in myself and you made my book shine with your fantastic input. I will be forever grateful to you.

To my beta readers. Your input, constructive criticism and encouragement made me realise I wasn't giving myself enough credit, so thank you for opening my eyes.

I would also like to thank Peter at Bespoke Book Covers who managed to capture the whole essence of the story in one image. It literally took my breath away.

Last but not least to my husband and children. Thank you so much for your support. This little book has been a labour of love and it was made all the more possible knowing that you all believed in me.

PROLOGUE

BEING WOKEN UP IN the middle of an already restless night is bad enough but now I'm looking at these two people, two police officers, on my doorstep. What the hell are the police doing here at this time of night? Christ, it's after one in the morning. I'm willing myself to wake up. It must be a bad dream. Yes, just a dream, their faces are going blurry…I must be waking up.

"Mrs Connor, I'm PC Stanton and this is my colleague PC Davies."

I can't see anymore. Where am I? I can hear voices, but I can't see. The voices sound like they are coming from the end of a tunnel. Oh God, I'm so scared. Where are you Aiden?

"Mrs Connor, Mrs Connor are you ok? Jesus… Mike radio control and get some medical help."

Who is Mike? There is only blackness now. I think I will sleep. Yes, sleep. Just sleep. See you in the morning Aiden.

***

"Hello ma'am, can you hear me? It's okay you're in safe hands."

Light flutters through my eyelids. This is one seriously weird dream.

"Can you open your eyes?" The voice sounds sweet and calming, female, not from around here. My eyes sting as they open and my head thumps.

"There we are. Can you tell me your name love?"

I see a mass of red curly hair as I take in my surroundings and realise I am in my own hallway. A flashing blue light emanates from behind the angel in green.

"Hey love, focus here." I hear clicking fingers and I follow the sound until I am looking into a beautiful set of jade green eyes.

"That's better, now what's your name?"

I can feel my mouth opening but the words don't come out. Gina Connor. Gina Connor. GINA CONNOR. My throat is so dry, I need water.

"…ink," I try to ask for some, but it comes out

wrong.

"Daz can you get the lady a drink of water?"

I hear footsteps.

"Right love we're getting you a glass of water. Do you know your name? Just signal with your head."

I nod. Northern Irish, that's her accent. Her voice is lovely, and she is very pretty.

"Right, here we are, take a drink of this." She holds the glass up to my mouth. My hands are shaking as I try to hold the glass and the water sloshes everywhere.

"It's alright I've got it. Try and take a few sips."

The cool water slides down my throat easily. As I close my eyes to savour it the glass is gone, and the snapping fingers return.

"Better?"

I nod.

"Right darlin' let's try again. What's your name?"

"Gina." Although a little croaky my vocal chords actually work and produce a viable sound.

"That's great Gina. What's your full name?"

"Gina Connor." I am aware of movement all around me, but I can't take my eyes off this woman.

"Right Gina. My name is Ava and I'm going to help you. Do you know where you are?"

"At home."

"That's great Gina. I'm just going to check you

over. You fainted and have a wee bump on your head. I need to make sure you don't have a concussion or anything serious. Is that okay?"

"Yes. Why did I faint, what happened?" I'm so confused, why are there all these emergency workers in my home? Where is Aiden?

"Where is my husband?" I ask Ava. The sympathetic sorrowful look on her face says it all. I know in my heart that something is wrong.

"Gina I just need to do a few little checks on you then these police officers need to speak to you okay?"

I am numb. My head nods but I don't feel it. I feel as though I am floating, watching everything from above, disconnected from my body, from my life. I am poked and prodded. Ava speaks to me and I answer automatically. As she finishes, I feel a sense of foreboding. I am led into the living room to sit somewhere more comfortable.

"Alright Gina honey that's me finished checking you out. You don't appear to have a concussion and all your vitals are fine. If you feel light headed or dizzy over the next 24 hours you need to get checked out, okay? Contact the A&E department at the hospital. Just because we don't see anything now doesn't mean that something won't crop up later."

I nod in response and she puts a hand on my shoulder and gives a little squeeze.

"The police need to speak to you, so I'll leave them to it."

As she moves away, I grab her arm. She turns and smiles. "I don't want to be alone," I whisper as I feel tears run down my face.

Ava puts her arm around my shoulder and pulls me in to her side. "I understand love. I'll stay until someone comes to be with you."

"Thank you Ava."

This woman doesn't know me from Adam but is willing to sit here as I break into a million pieces. Looking down at my hands I notice that I am clutching my left hand in my right and squeezing my wedding ring tight, giving it a little twist every few seconds. I feel Ava tense and looking up I notice the two police officers from earlier approach me. I am shaking and finding it hard to breathe.

"It's okay Gina I'm here, you have to stay calm. Breathe in deeply and let it out slowly." Ava's soothing voice calms me enough to listen when the officer starts talking.

"Mrs Connor, my name is Shaun Stanton. I'm a family liaison officer. This is my colleague Mike Davies. Is your husband Aiden Connor?"

I nod.

"Mrs Connor I'm really sorry but I have to inform you that Aiden was involved in a serious accident this evening. Emergency services were called and arrived within a few minutes but there was nothing they could do, and he was pronounced dead at the scene."

I can't hear what else he is saying. There is a high-pitched animal-like wailing ringing in my ears. It takes me a few seconds to realise that sound is coming from me. Oh God, this cannot be happening. What am I going to do?

"Gina," Ava says quietly. "We've had a call in and I need to go. You're in good hands here and your mum is on her way okay? I'm so sorry for your loss honey. Stay strong and remember to get medical help if you feel you need it."

Ava's eyes are teary. All I can muster is a quiet thank you. Moments later she is gone and I am left alone with the two police officers. There is an eerie silence between us all as I try to absorb what has happened. My whole world has imploded, my heart shattered. I feel numb. My whole reason for being is gone.

CHAPTER 1

Six Months Later

I HAVE NEVER THOUGHT of myself as pretty, at least not compared to the beautiful celebs and models that are splashed all over the media. I am average, normal and look ok with a bit of make-up on. My long brown hair and blue eyes are a bonus and I have curves in the right places. I know I will never be a svelte size 8 it's just not in my genes. I am healthy and that's all that matters to me. My husband thought I was beautiful, I think he was biased. He always made me feel loved and wanted. If I felt terrible he would always do or say something to make me laugh. Anything from funky facial expressions to putting dirty words into songs and singing them out loud to me.

The last six months have been hard, and grief has taken its toll on me. I feel older than my 31 years; damn it I look older. Catching a glimpse of myself in the mirror on my dressing table I feel tears start to well up from my heart, a heart that is still pained every time I look at my empty bed. I close my eyes against the stinging of the salt water. I can see Aiden walking in and wrapping me up in a big bear hug, telling me I am beautiful. I squeeze my eyes tight sending trickles down my cheeks. In the distance the revving of a car engine brings me out of my reverie and I open my eyes. I look at the mirror and there is only me with my arms wrapped round myself painfully wishing that he was here. I miss him so much.

It is just after midday and I have to get ready for my weekly grilling by Dr. Nathan Dempsey (Nate), my therapist, who is not much older than me. I think that is why I have stuck with him for so long. He is easy to talk to and doesn't rush me or dismiss me. I never wanted to go in the first place. I didn't think I needed it, but I had gone to keep Dr. Parsons off my back and stop him from prescribing anti-depressants. I am not depressed, I have too many other things to occupy my mind to be depressed, or so I like to keep telling myself. The good doctor had come to see me a week after Aiden's funeral, I highly suspect at the insistence of my mother-in-law, and sat looking at me with pity over his thin wire glasses. He is possibly in his late 50's and always looks like he got dressed in the dark. He told me that the reality of my 'situation' had not yet hit me and that I should try to speak to someone. Apparently, I have a mild case of Post-Traumatic Stress Disorder. I thought that happened to people who had been in an accident or had witnessed something terrible or had experienced some sort of physical trauma, so when it was directed at me, I was shocked. It took another few weeks of persuasion and threats of the dreaded 'Happy Pills' before I finally agreed. It was only an hour a week on a Tuesday afternoon. I really didn't have any excuse not to go and Dr. Parsons knew it. He knew I didn't have any children or commitments.

Aiden had said he wanted to wait for our careers to take off before we started a family. I have a degree in business and economics, but photography was my passion and I had aspired to be a hot shot photojournalist, travelling the world photographing the rich and famous, stunning places and interesting people. My dream was to live and work in New York. Turns out there are too many people already doing that and I was a bottom feeder compared to most of them. I found my vocation doing portraits from my little studio in the high street. I photographed weddings, parties and other social events. In the end I had to give up the studio and have fallen into a rut since, I have no motivation to photograph happy people. My poor camera is neglected. Aiden qualified in structural engineering and was destined for great things. He got a part time surveyors job at the local council offices while he waited for his big break. Part-time turned into full-time and as he moved up the ranks he found it harder to honour his aspirations. We had discussed having kids but there was always something going on and it never seemed like the right time. A part of me now thinks it was just as well we didn't, I don't know how I would have coped on my own with a kid; I can barely keep myself going. Who knew we were not going to be together forever? We thought we had all the time in the world. I was comfortably complacent and oblivious to the fragility of life and it was ripped from me in a few short minutes by the side of a country road.

So, here I am off to talk to Nate for an hour to see if he can help. I usually take the bus in to town on a Tuesday afternoon because parking is highly coveted and costs an arm and a leg if you are lucky enough to get a space. Nate's office is in a tall sandstone building with large sash windows and a beautiful set of pillars on either side of the main door. It is in the west end of Glasgow, a very affluent part of the city, near the University and sits inconspicuously on a tree lined avenue overlooking Kelvingrove Park. I sometimes take a stroll through the park before I go home just to clear my head.

There are 3 floors in the building. The two offices on the ground floor belong to a private dentist. I always grin as I pass and see the little set of teeth on legs smiling at me from the sign on the front door, 'Sparkles Dental Practice'. I have never seen the dentist, but I imagine her to be tall, blonde and perfectly groomed wearing a pink uniform with diamantes spelling out her name. My imagination is ridiculous; *it's not a beauty salon for God's sake*. Just above the teeth on legs is a new sign I haven't noticed before. It would appear that they now do Botox. This makes me laugh. From the look of me today I should probably keep this in mind, I may get to meet 'Dr. Sparkles' after all. An architect and an accounts consultant occupy the second floor. They don't have funky names. The architect is S. Parker and the accountant is D. Todd, not a lot to imagine there. The only images I can conjure up are two short, bald, old guys who look exactly the same wearing the same bland suit sitting behind identical desks. This floor is far too boring for my liking.

I arrive at my destination, on the third floor, and am greeted by Nate's receptionist and my once a week impartial friend Fiona. She has blonde curls to her shoulders and a flawless complexion like a little china doll. She is always cheerful and has a smile for everyone. Then again, I would always have a smile on my face too if I worked with Nate, he is an extremely handsome man and Fiona's husband.

"Oh, hi Gina," Fiona chirps, her beaming smile makes me smile as well. Apparently it's infectious.

"Hi Fiona, looking lovely as ever," I reply, she always looks perfectly preened.

"Oh you're too kind Gina. You look happy today, it's nice to see your smile."

"I just saw the sign on the dentist's door on my way in and it made me laugh."

"Oh the Botox! Nate had a laugh at that on the way in this morning too and the cheeky sod told me that I should bear it in mind. I may be husbandless by the end of the day…Oh I'm so sorry Gina, the words were out before I knew what I was saying," Fiona cries as she clamps her hand over her mouth.

I flash her my biggest smile to reassure her as inside my heart sinks. I hate people walking on eggshells around me. "Fiona don't apologise, I'm fine. I'm early today, is Nate with someone just now?"

"Thank you Gina, I'll try and link my brain to my mouth in future. He's with a new client right now so the session may overrun a bit"

Her eyes are so full of apology, I could never have been mad at her even if I wanted to, she's just so lovely.

"No problem, I'm going to go and grab a bite to eat at the deli on the corner. Would you like me to get you anything?" Thinking back to my first session with Nate I know I could be waiting a while.

"No thanks, I've already had lunch and if I drink any more coffee I'm likely to pee myself right here in this chair." We both have a chuckle at that as I head for the door.

"See you shortly."

As I reach the front door of the building, I can feel the cold, end of November air greeting me with its harsh bite. I pull my coat around me and tighten my scarf then proceed out onto the steps. I have my head down fishing in my pockets for my gloves when I feel an almighty thud hit me square on. My head shoots up just in time to see a brown-haired figure in an expensive looking grey three-piece suit tumble down the stairs. Jesus…he is gorgeous. This should not be my first thought after knocking him down the stairs but…WOW! He has eyes like Paul Newman with a bit of young Marlon Brando thrown in for good measure. His skin is slightly tanned, and he is clean-shaven. His hair is so perfectly styled it looks like it wouldn't move even in a tornado.

"Oh my God I am so sorry, are you ok?" I rush to his side and put my hand on his arm, oh my, what a nice arm that is. I feel a little buzz and the hairs on my arms stand to attention, as do other parts of my anatomy. I immediately let go, shocked at my reaction.

"I didn't even hear you I'm so sorry." My voice is uncharacteristically high, and I am talking too fast, but I can't seem to control myself. What the hell is wrong with me? *'Get a Goddamn grip Gina he's just a man…gorgeous but just a man.'*

As he gathers himself and his briefcase up, he looks at me with the most beautiful deep blue eyes I have ever seen. He holds my gaze, I can't tear my eyes away, I am mesmerised.

"Please be more careful in future missy, you could have caused some serious damage there." He looks at me like I am a naughty child being told off for running in the school corridor with an open pair of scissors. I don't know what to say. How bloody dare you, you cheeky bastard. Missy, MISSY! He doesn't even know me. As I stand there seething at this complete stranger's total dismissal of me, he turns on his heel and walks into the building without a

20

backward glance. All I can manage is a shake of my head as I stand there in utter disbelief. I can feel tears well beneath my lids. '*Stop it right now Gina, he is not worth it,*' I tell myself without much conviction. I apologised for goodness sake. What did he want me to do? Fall to my knees and beg his forgiveness like he was some sort of God. He was rather hot and, as much as I hate to admit it, those eyes were amazing but like most hot guys he was full of himself. I hope his butt cheeks hurt...moron. He is probably having the accountant on the second floor fiddle his books. Although the exchange only took five minutes I feel as though I have been outside for an hour. I am freezing and not even hungry anymore...I am too mad. I decide to go back inside and have a coffee in the waiting room, scowling and sticking my fingers up at the accountant's door on my way past.

CHAPTER 2

MY SESSION WITH NATE goes well. As usual we discuss how I am feeling, how I am filling my days, whether or not I am seeing friends and family, am I keeping active and the like. I respond automatically. I am fine, I am going to the gym, swimming, reading etc., seeing my friends and my mum a few times a week. Of course, none of this is true, I just don't have the energy and I only speak to people on the phone now and again. In actual fact my only real human face-to-face interaction is with Nate and Fiona every Tuesday. I had so many visitors in the days following the accident and after the funeral that I just wanted peace and quiet. I thought that would only last a few weeks, but it seems to have become routine now, I actually like my own company. I suspect that Nate knows I am lying; he wouldn't be very good at his job if he didn't. I am sure he is humouring me at the moment. In all honesty I enjoy our little hour together, it's good to talk to someone who doesn't pity me all the time.

It is now 3.30pm and the sky has a mauve hue to it. I don't like the winter nights and the closer it gets to Christmas the more I hate them. Aiden and I used to cosy up with each other on these cold dark nights after we had spent the day Christmas shopping in town. This year Christmas can take a hike, I am not interested. I am lost in my thoughts as I walk towards the bus stop. Looking up I notice a tall man with his back to me. He is wearing a black overcoat and is fighting with his briefcase lock next to an absolutely stunning jet-black Aston Martin. The registration plate is simple: SP1. Very expensive. I didn't notice it earlier, I would have remembered since it is my dream car and that plate is hard to miss. As I get closer the click click click of my heels makes him turn and look in my direction. My heart constricts, oh Jesus Christ, it is that moron from earlier. I don't want another confrontation, so I look down at the ground and walk faster. I really want to punch the bastard, but I don't want to get myself arrested.

"Excuse me." The voice calls to me. I carry on

walking. Fuck you asshole, I am not in the mood.

"EXCUSE ME!" Much louder this time. Still I ignore him.

"Excuse me MISSY!" He is laughing now. That's it, I stop abruptly and spin on my heel ready to take aim and knock the idiot to his arse again.

"Do not EVER call me Missy again you condescending bastard," I shout at him. I must look like a mental case bawling at a complete stranger in the street. I try my best to control myself, but I can already feel the tears welling up in my eyes and I know it won't be long before it all comes flooding out. I am shaking, not from the cold, from pent up emotion.

When I look at him again, he is still smiling and that tips me over the edge. My mind detaches itself from my body and before I know what I am doing I lift my hand and crack him on the jaw with a slap that makes some birds in the tree across the street from us take flight. My legs choose that moment to give up on me and I collapse in a heap on the cold hard ground, sobbing uncontrollably with my head in my hands. I feel him kneel down beside me and put his arm around me. He is warm and smells so good that I want to snuggle in to him; then I remember he is a cheeky bastard and is the reason I am now slumped on the pavement. But, then again, would a complete moron comfort a crazy lady who had just slapped him in the middle of the street? I look up at him and into those deep blue eyes and feel like I could get lost in them.

"Are you ok?" His voice is sincere and not as harsh as it had sounded in our earlier exchange.

"I'm fine." I really don't have anything else to say to him and I am slightly embarrassed. I really don't think he deserved to be slapped like that. Now I feel like such a bitch. He helps me up and brushes off my coat for me. He gently moves my hair, which has got stuck in my tears, from my face. As his hand brushes my skin, I feel a little buzz again. I close my eyes and savour it.

When I open them he is looking at me, smile gone, with his face full of concern. Good God he is gorgeous, I can't take my eyes off his beautiful features. Holding out his hand for me I gratefully accept, happy to get off the cold damp ground.

"I have to apologise for the way I spoke to you earlier, I'm so sorry. I thought the 'missy thing' had annoyed you that's the only reason I used it. I knew you were going to ignore me, but I really didn't expect to get a slap for it; I thought you would see the funny side. I was in a rush earlier after an exceptionally heated meeting with a client, so I was not in the best frame of mind when we bumped into each other." His voice is lovely and calming and not patronising at all. I can feel my face flush crimson.

"Yes, I'm sorry for that, is your cheek okay?"

"I'll live I'm sure."

He holds out his hand in a handshake gesture, "My name is Steven by the way."

I take his hand; his big warm hand and give it a little shake.

"Georgina... eh Gina." Damn, I can't believe I gave my Sunday name first. Only my mum uses my full name. I am starting to feel giddy at his touch. Am I a bloody hormonal teenager or a grown woman?

"Well nice to meet you Gina. I assume you are heading home; would you like a lift?" I look at Steven's face and his smile is back, softer this time and without an ounce of pity.

"No, it's fine, really, I can catch the bus it goes right past my house." I really don't think I should accept a lift from a complete stranger. He could be a raving lunatic using his charm and flash car to lure unsuspecting females to his lair.

"Are you sure? It's cold and dark and I don't think my conscience will let me leave you to get home on your own" And there it is, the patronising voice again as if I am a fragile little girl and can't get myself home. I am not amused.

"You can drop me at the bus stop and wait till my

bus arrives if that makes you feel better." That's my compromise. He is a stranger so the bus stop where there are other people about will do nicely. My mind is going into overdrive playing scenarios of me being found chained up in his basement after being tortured to death. I have honestly got to stop watching gory horrors on my own this is getting ridiculous.

"Good, at least I'll know you're safe. This street is a bit creepy when you can't see into the park, you just never know what strange people are lurking in there." His smile reaches his eyes. The street is now dimly lit with the orange glow of street lamps but even in this subdued light I can see he is very knicker rippingly gorgeous.

"Shall we?" He grins hooking out his arm in an 'I'm a Little Teapot' fashion. I take his arm and we walk to his car.

Steven presses a button on the remote and the interior lights up. From where I am standing, I can see the seats are black with bright red stitching. The gear paddle on the steering column is covered in red leather. The luxuriousness of it all has me conjuring up scenes of espionage, car chases and a man who knows how to handle the ladies. The red against black is enchanting, very James Bond-esque. I shake my head and banish those thoughts. '*Enough*,' I scold myself; '*you've just been to therapy because your husband just died'.* Steven opens the door for me; very charming, probably one of his ploys. I smile at my over active imagination.

"What's so funny?"

"Oh nothing, I was just admiring your car it's very nice."

"It's an Ast..."

"Aston Martin, I know it's actually my dream car." Damn, as if his head isn't big enough already. He is smiling like a child who has been locked in a sweet shop overnight. Boys and their toys. Aiden was the same whenever he talked about his bike. That damn death trap that got him killed. With a slight shake of my head I return to the here and now. I get into the car as ladylike as I can in heels and a dress; the seats are so low that I think I may have flashed my knickers slightly. Judging by the look on Steven's face that is most likely. I blush; thank God it's dark.

Removing his overcoat and suit jacket Steven throws them onto the back seat along with his briefcase. He looks even better in his shirt, tie and waistcoat. I feel a familiar sensation between my legs and abruptly squeeze them shut to try and stop it as the car roars to life. I can feel it rumble beneath me and, oh my God, that is just making things worse. I try to find something to distract me and settle on watching Steven press icons on the little touch screen which has magically appeared from the dash board. His iPhone is showing as connected and a multitude of playlists come up on the screen. He selects one named 'driving music'. The speakers' spring to life and the car is filled with a beautiful and calming sound. I recognise the soft piano music from various TV ads and programmes. Any man who likes this type of music surely can't be an axe murderer. *'Although Hannibal Lector enjoyed his fair share of classical music'*. I swear I am going to give myself a stroke.

"This music is nice," I whisper; I don't dare to look at him for fear I may implode.

"Yeah, great for relaxing you after a hard day."

I feel him looking at me and am compelled to turn and face him. He has a boyish grin on his face which is making him look even hotter. I smile involuntarily. Holding my gaze for a moment Steven says: "You have a beautiful smile Gina."

Oh bugger, where the hell did that come from? I quickly turn my head away and look out the window again. My face is flushed, not because I didn't like what he said but because I did. Steven reaches over and puts his fingers on my chin forcing my face back towards him.

"What's wrong?" His voice is full of concern, tinged with worry that he may have said something wrong. His touch pulses through my skin. I have to get out of here.

"My bus will be on its way. Can you please take me to the bus stop?" It comes out all harsh and wrong; I need to keep a clear head. Steven looks wounded at my sudden change in demeanour.

"Not a problem," he says dryly. We get to the bus stop in record time and in silence. The purr of the car's engine and the soft strains of the piano are all we can hear.

"Thanks for the lift Steven and I'm sorry again for the slap."

I give him one last look and before he can say anything I am out of the car and standing in the queue. The other people waiting in line are all gawping at the stunning vehicle I have just alighted. I can see the headlights of the bus approaching and start praying that it will get here before he has the chance to get out and talk to me again. I am a little shocked and disheartened that he doesn't even look at me, speeding off in a blur. Not even a goodbye wave. Deep down I was hoping he would beg me to get back into the car. What I was hoping would happen after that I don't know but right now I am reeling at how stupid I have just been. For goodness sake I don't even know his last name or anything about him except that he drives the most beautiful machine and likes piano music. Oh, and he is seriously hot. He could be one of the strangers waiting for the bus; I probably know more about them. As the bus pulls to a stop I think about that for a moment. The old lady getting on first is a regular. She only travels two stops, but I have spoken to her on a few occasions and I know that her name is Martha. Her husband died twelve years ago, and she has no children or other immediate family. Just her friend down the road and her wee dog. Good God I could be looking at my future looking at her.

I take my usual seat right at the back. It has started to spit with rain and the windows of the bus are steamy. I can see the outline of a heart with initials in it. It makes me think of being in love as a teenager; little did we know how cruel life and love really is. I am destined to be alone like Martha. I feel like such an idiot. Steven seemed really nice and I blew it because I'm fucked up. I don't even know if I will ever see him again. Something changes in me at that very moment. It is like a little light has been turned on inside me as I realise that things need to change. Right now, in fact. I get off the bus at the stop next to the train station. The rain has gotten heavier and is now turning to sleet. Oh, winter is definitely here. Inside the station I am faced with that familiar diesel fuel and sulphur smell mixed with coffee and cookies.

The overhead display boards show that the train I am looking for is on time and will leave in 12 minutes. Just enough time to get a coffee and head to the platform. As I get closer to the Starbucks kiosk the smell of the freshly ground coffee makes me feel warm inside. I wish coffee could cure everything.

"Welcome to Starbucks, how can I help you today?" Says the overly happy barista whose badge is telling me she is named Lucia.

"Skinny Mocha please." I smile back. "Just a small one thanks."

"What's your name for the order?" She asks holding the iconic white cup in one hand and a Sharpie in the other.

"Gina."

My hands are cold, even inside my gloves, so when she hands me the coffee I am grateful. The steam coming from the little drinking hole is comforting. I can actually feel myself smile. I look at my name on the cup and see that Lucia has put a little heart next to it with a smiley face inside it; my smile becomes even wider.

"Have a nice day," Lucia beams.

"You too, thanks."

I wonder, for a moment, what someone like Lucia would have done in my situation. She looks about 20, a student more than likely, I bet she would never have run for the hills at the drop of a hat; but then would any student? I used to be one, I know what they are like.

As I make my way to the platform, I pull out my phone and call the one person I know who will make me feel better. The phone is answered on the third ring.

"Hello?" The voice on the other end makes me feel like I am being wrapped up in a fleece blanket.

"Hello mum, how are you?"

"Oh Georgina! How lovely to hear from you. I'm wonderful. Dad is off to pick up some take away because I can't be bothered cooking tonight and he has some project or something to work on. Oh darling I've missed you. How long has it been since I last saw you? Three weeks or longer, my goodness we need to catch up before I forget what you look like. Where are you it sounds busy?"

That's my mum, once she starts talking it takes a while for you to get a word in.

"I'm in the train station mum, just about to get on the train to Bearsden. I was just calling to make sure you were home."

"Oh, that's wonderful, I'll try and catch Dad and get him to bring more food. Is Chinese ok?"

I try to tell her I am not hungry, but it is in vain, she just keeps going. She mentions something about a

33

new car and my cousin being pregnant before I can eventually get off the phone and get on the train.

I choose a seat near the doors facing the direction I'm travelling in. I have always felt weird travelling backwards. It is after rush hour now, so the train is not that busy. I pull my earphones out of my pocket and plug them into my iPhone. Shuffling the playlist I go for a lucky dip. The song that comes on makes me think about earlier today. A song called Runaway: *'Take your time; don't go running away from this.'* Yes, that's what I did, I ran away from something that scared me. It shouldn't have but it's been so long since I felt like that around anyone else that I didn't know how to handle the situation. Now Steven probably thinks I am a lunatic. You win some, you lose some but losing this one has had an effect on me. I can't stop thinking about him.

CHAPTER 3

THE TWENTY MINUTE JOURNEY to my parent's house seems quicker than normal and as I get off the train, I see that the sleet has turned to snow. I love how light everything seems when it is snowing; everything seems brighter even though it is dark. I am glad I am on foot; I really don't like driving in the snow. I do, however, wish I had boots on and not high heels. Thank goodness the walk to mum and dad's is only five minutes I may end up with frostbite otherwise.

My family home is in a 'posh' suburb of Glasgow where the lawns are perfectly manicured, and the cars are all high spec. My parents are both retired but are still only in their fifties, the prime of their lives as my mum puts it. They both had great careers and retired early. Mum was a partner in a law firm in the city and dad was a structural engineer who became a lecturer at Glasgow University. Aiden was a top student in one of dad's classes. If Aiden had turned out anything like my dad, I would have been very lucky. You couldn't get a better man than my dad. He is the perfect husband and father. As I approach the wrought iron gates at the entrance of the driveway the sight that greets me almost knocks me flat on my back. Sitting at the top of the drive is a jet-black Aston Martin with a thin layer of snow on top. Surely not? What sort of freaky fucked up coincidence would that be? The snow is getting heavier and I notice the number plate on the back is snowed over. I wipe the snow off and pull back sharply, the number plate reads 'SP1'. Oh bloody hell. I don't know whether to run or hide. My heart is doing back flips and I realise I have a smile on my face. What the hell is he doing here, at my parents' house of all places? I wonder for a fleeting second if maybe he is a stalker.

Hesitantly I open the large wooden internal door. I try to be as quiet as possible but Clio, my mum's Miniature Schnauzer, gives me away as she comes flying at me like a bat out of hell. The yip yip yipping alerts everyone. Mum emerges from the kitchen and her eyes light up like Christmas. Throwing her arms out she shouts: "Oh my baby girl come and give me a hug!"

"Hi mum." I smile and hug her with all I have. I really have missed her. In the last six months I have only seen her a handful of times and even then, I wasn't really there.

"Oh darling, let's get you warmed up, your feet must be freezing." She ushers me into the kitchen, with Clio still running around my heels, and before I can say anything she is off on one, it's like I've never been away.

"So, Aunt May called me this morning to tell me that your cousin Leah is pregnant. She is four months gone and didn't even know, I mean how can you not know? I know I only had you, but you do know, it's so obvious. She is in shock because," she leans in close to me with her hand to the side of her mouth thinking she is whispering. "She doesn't even know who the father is. May is disgusted and has asked that we keep it under wraps. I won't let on to anyone, but I always said that girl would be trouble, that's what happens when children are left to their own devices."

My Aunt May, my father's older sister, thinks her children are angels and never had a good word to say about me when I was younger. My cousin Leah was her third child and was conceived when May was 44. She thought it was the menopause but got the shock of her life when she discovered this condition came with arms and legs. Leah was given everything she wanted and was never told off for anything. She is now 19 and only started University in September. She is one year into a four-year degree in Psychology. I wonder how the little princess will cope. I am acutely aware that Steven is in this house somewhere.

"...Mercedes. He is having a delayed midlife crisis I think, don't you?"

Good grief, she has been talking nonstop for about ten minutes.

"Sorry mum I got side tracked there, who is having a midlife crisis?"

"Your father, were you not listening to me? He has gone and bought himself a new car. A Mercedes of all things. A sporty little number, he calls it, with only two seats. I mean who buys a car like that when they are about to go headfirst into their 60's? Would you like a glass of wine darling? There is plenty of food, I managed to get hold of dad before he made it to the take away. The new car has Bluetooth, so he can talk on the phone hands free; gadgets these days are incredible."

"Maybe he just feels like a change mum. Anyway, I think you will look cool driving a car like that." We both have a laugh at that because we know it will be his baby and he won't let anyone else drive it.

"I would love a glass of wine, thanks mum."

I am conscious of movement out in the hallway. Dad's office door closes with a thud followed by muffled voices. As I turn to look at the kitchen door, I nearly fall off the bar stool when mum's voice screeches from behind me: "Martin your beloved daughter is here."

From behind her hand she whispers: "He's having a little business deal with some hotshot architect." Raising her eyebrows, she gives me a little wink. "He used to be one of his students, very handsome and drives a very nice car. Did you see it on the way in?"

This is too much to take in right now and I am sitting there in shock when my father comes through the door. I quickly turn away before Steven sees me; my face is as scarlet as the colour in his car.

"Oh my beautiful girlie, how are you my darling?" Dad says as he hugs me so tight I think my eyes might explode.

"I'm good dad." I turn and look towards the door, but no one is there.

"Who were you talking to dad?" I say as calmly as I can and am only slightly betrayed by the high-pitched tone of my voice.

"Oh that was Steven one of my old students. He graduated a few years ago and has his own very successful business now. We were discussing a

39

project he is working on."

Mum looks at him with that accusatory glare and he gives a half smile and says: "I know, Carla, I know. I'm supposed to be relaxing and enjoying retirement, but I still like to keep my hand in you know. Come and meet him Gina he's a nice young man."

Before I can even hesitate, he has me off the stool and into the hallway. Steven has his back to us looking at the pictures on the wall; pictures of me as a child. Oh wonderful! This day just keeps getting better. His hands are in his pockets stretching the material over a very tight bum. '*Oh, get your mind out of the gutter Gina*'. He looks perfect with his tailored, toned physique and beautiful hair. I want to touch him so much right now.

"Steven come and meet my daughter," Dad says as Steven turns to look at me. The expression on his face would be funny if this wasn't actually happening. Shock, confusion and amusement all rolled into one. "This is Gina, Gina this is Steven Parker. He was one of my most, shall we say, outspoken students."

Steven Parker? Oh my God, S. Parker, the architect in Nate's building. I didn't even make the connection with the registration plate. Wow, nothing old bald and boring about him. I am having a hard time making sense of everything. I think if my brain had been a computer it would be displaying the blue screen of death by now. Steven gives a little laugh and nods in my direction.

"Hi Gina, nice to meet you, nice pictures by the way." He smiles, gesturing towards the pictures as he holds out his hand. I offer mine in return but instead of a handshake he grazes my knuckles with a delicate kiss. A buzz shoots through me making me gasp; my face flushes as I try to remain calm. What my dad says next makes me happy, scared and uncomfortable all at once.

"Would you like to stay for some food Steven? There is plenty to go round."

"That would be lovely Martin, thank you," Steven says as he smiles directly at me and I think I am about to expire.

"Fantastic, I'll go and let Carla know to set another place."

As my dad leaves, Steven slowly caresses my body with his eyes. There is no sound except my laboured breathing until the silence is finally broken by Steven: "So, this is fun huh?"

I am unable to speak.

"Gina, I'm sorry about earlier. I shouldn't have left like that, but you didn't seem to want me around." The sincerity in his eyes is heart melting and I am totally mesmerised.

"No, I'm sorry. I'm not used to a man looking at me like you did or speaking to me like that. I panicked. When you drove off, I was pissed off with myself because I didn't know if I would see you again. It's been a long time since I felt this way about a guy, I don't know what to say or do. It's really weird that you're here, at my parent's house, on the same day I choose to visit. Things like this just don't happen".

Pointing to a photograph of me in my wedding dress Steven answers: "So, I didn't realise you were married, I didn't notice your rings earlier."

This was not a conversation I wanted to have today, not when I am trying to put the past to rest.

"I was married for 5 years. We were together for 10," I say keeping my head down because I know if I look up the floodgates will open.

"Was? Did he leave you?"

"You could say that, he died six months ago. His motorbike was hit head on by a drunk driver four times over the limit and doing twice the speed limit. I still wear my rings because I can't bear to take them off. These are the only things I have left that he gave to me." I feel tears run down my cheeks. Great, I am going to look wonderful now.

"Oh my God, I'm so sorry."

"Don't be, it's not your problem. I don't want your pity." I am being a bitch again, but I hate people feeling sorry for me.

"It's not pity, I truly am sorry for your loss, it must have been hard. You said you were married for 5 years, together for 10? I hope you don't slap me again for asking this, but how old are you?" As soon as he asks the question he moves back ever so slightly. This makes me smile. I like the U-turn.

"Thirty-one, and I should knock you out you know. It's extremely rude to ask a lady her age."

"That saying is only true when a man is talking to a LADY!" It comes out like layyydeee and that is it, I am laughing hard now. I give him a punch on the arm.

"That's not nice," I say, putting on my best pouty face. I fold my arms across my chest like a sulky child though I cannot contain my smile. When I look at him, he is smiling too.

"What?" I ask trying not to seem too amused but failing miserably.

"You don't look your age you know. I would have said you looked about 25, if that. You're very beautiful Gina and I mean that."

Oh how on earth do I handle this? In my mind Aiden is giving me the thumbs up. I know he would want me to be happy and right now I actually am

43

happy. I smile shyly.

"Thanks, that's very flattering," I say still a little cautiously.

"We better get in there before they send out a search party…or the dog."

"Sure thing, I'm starving."

His smile is fantastic, I could get lost in it. I grab his arm before we reach the kitchen door. "Can we please not let on to them that we know each other? I really don't want any awkward questions."

"Not a problem, I can do discreet." He leans in close to me and whispers in my ear: "They will never know what exceptionally naughty things I want to do to their daughter."

His breath on my skin makes the hairs on my neck stand on end and sends a shiver down my spine. His words make my insides jump. He wants to do EXCEPTIONALLY naughty things to me. I am a little shocked and very turned on by it all. I try to compose myself; this could be an interesting night.

CHAPTER 4

I'VE HAD A LITTLE too much to drink. I'm not drunk but my head is a bit fuzzy. It's as though I have been transported into someone else's life. Over dinner Steven managed to slot right in to our family. He has been laughing and joking with dad and charming mum who is lapping up his compliments like she is fifteen again. I have even found myself joining in with the jovial atmosphere and I realise that this is just what I needed today. If I am going to push my life in a new direction, why not start now, why not start with him?

"Looks like that snow is on for the night folks," Dad says as he gets up from the table and crosses to the window that is all fogged up from the heat in the kitchen.

"Oh Georgina I really don't want you going home alone in that weather, you stay here tonight, and dad will take you home in the morning," Mum says with her over protective mother-hen voice.

"Mum I'll be fine, I'm a big girl you know, I can look after myself." I smile at her concern. I am, after all, her only child.

"I can drop you home if you like Georgina? You don't live far do you?"

Oh you shit, trying to get in mum's good books by using my proper name. What do I say to that?

Before I can answer dad pipes up. "Don't think you will be going anywhere either Steven, not unless you want to dig your car out first."

Steven joins dad at the kitchen window. "Oh dear Martin it looks like an igloo."

He turns to me wearing a smile like the Cheshire Cat. My insides are churning. The look he is giving me has something else written all over it and I am shocked to find myself enjoying it.

"Right that settles it you're both staying here, we have plenty of room. I won't be held responsible for sending you home in the snow and for you to have an accident. I couldn't live with myself." Mum is talking so fast it may be impossible to understand her soon. I look over at Steven who is smiling at me, his eyes full of mischief.

"Thank you Mrs Harper, but only if you are sure." He has not taken his eyes off me and I almost collapse when he discreetly winks at me.

"Not another word about it. Georgina go and sort out one of the spare rooms for Steven. You know where everything is. You can sort out your own room too, we redecorated it last month and I think you'll like it."

I take the opportunity to escape before I crumble under Steven's gaze. I have to remain calm and focused, I am only spending the night at my parent's house and there just happens to be a houseguest too. Yes that's all he is just a houseguest.

As I make my way from the kitchen up the hallway to the stairs, I am reminded how much I miss being here. I have so many happy memories of growing up in this beautiful house, on this beautiful street, with the best parents in the world. The house is huge with five bedrooms and seven bathrooms. I always thought it extravagant for just us, but mum and dad didn't buy it, they inherited it from one of my dad's great aunts who never married and had no children. When she was too frail to look after herself mum and dad moved in with her and became her carers until she died. They were like the children she longed to have and so the house was her way of saying thank you. I don't remember her, I was only a baby when she passed away, but mum said she was a wonderful, worldly woman and it was because of her that she decided to become a career woman. They loved the house so much that they never intended to move and the condition for me to inherit it when they are no longer here is that I never sell it. It has to stay in the family and that is fine by me, I love this house too.

My old bedroom is at the back of the house and overlooks the huge garden. Mum and dad have replaced all the doors in the house since I have last been here. Gone are the white doors and white facings. Everything is a lovely warm oak colour now to match the staircase, it is very welcoming and cosy. I am pleasantly surprised when I open the door. My old butterfly wallpaper has been painted white on three walls with a beautiful dark plum colour as a feature wall. A large warm oak king size bed stands where my little four poster single bed used to, my little princess bed. All the furniture matches the bed and there is a flat screen TV on the wall. Wow, mum you really did well in here, I smile to myself. The bathroom has been designed as a wet room with white and plum tiles. Matching towels festoon the heated towel rail and there are some little Chanel toiletries next to the sink. It reminds me of a posh boutique hotel. Yes, I like it.

I go into the room next door and realise all the bedrooms have had a bit of a makeover. This one has teal accents. Mum must be getting sick of wallpaper because the walls have all been painted in here too. This used to be my grandmothers' room when she came to stay and was, the last time I saw it, very old lady like. Flowers adorned every surface; wallpaper, bedding, curtains, carpet. She even had flowery drawer liners. It was her home from home. It used to smell like her. I close my eyes, I miss you gran. Snapping out of my daydream I turn quickly and see Steven standing in the doorway regarding me with a smirk on his face.

"Hi," I say tentatively. His smile broadens, and I see a flash of white teeth. I wonder for a second if he visits Dr Sparkles and I am surprised to find a touch of jealousy wash over me. What the hell? I shake my head slightly to banish that stupid thought. He is holding his shoes in one hand and his briefcase in the other. His coat and jacket are draped perfectly over his arm. I am about to have a nervous breakdown.

"Hi yourself. Is this my room?"

"Yes. There are fresh sheets on the bed and toiletries in the bathroom. Mum always keeps new toothbrushes in the cupboards. They get a lot of overnight guests."

Walking in, Steven closes the door, puts his coat and jacket on the tub chair in the corner and lays his briefcase down beside it. His shoes are placed neatly under the front of the chair. He sits down on the bed and bounces slightly to test it. Patting the space beside him he says: "Come here Gina, I have something I need to tell you."

Oh God, this sounds ominous. I do as I am asked and sit beside him as far away as I can without being rude. Oh my, he smells divine, a mixture of aftershave and man. Pausing to gather his thoughts I sense a nervous energy coming from him. Funny, he didn't strike me as the nervous type when we first 'bumped' into each other.

"Gina, I've been watching you every week for the last 5 months going in and out of my building. The first time I saw you I wanted to touch you. I couldn't wait for 2 o'clock on a Tuesday afternoon because I knew I would see you. Today I was rushing back from my meeting because I thought I was going to miss you. When we ran in to each other I was so shocked when you touched me that I just had to get out of there."

Looking down at his feet his cheeks flush a little red. Good God he has been watching me! The Police song 'Every Breath You Take' springs to mind. I could take this as the behaviour of a stalker.

However, I feel a warm glow at the fact that he has been obsessed with me. I don't know if it is wrong or just self-indulgent, but it makes me feel good.

"You've been watching me?" I finally say.

"I know I sound like a stalker, but I never did anything to find out who you were, or anything so please don't think I'm a weirdo." He has a little crooked smile on his face and it is so sexy.

"It was like winning the lottery tonight when I realised I was actually in your parents' house and you were here too, the world really is a small place. Do you believe in 'meant to be' Gina? I do, and I think this was meant to be."

"I often wondered what you and your neighbour on the second floor looked like. I'm sorry to say in my mind you were both short, bald, old and boring." I smile and blush at the same time. His laugh is so hearty and his eyes sparkle.

"Well I hope you are pleasantly surprised, and by the way Donald, my neighbour, is short, bald, old and boring."

I am laughing now as well and am startled when he reaches out to touch my cheek. I close my eyes and savour his touch. The familiar buzz intensifies and the sensation is coursing through me like an electric current.

"Mmmm."

I murmur and press my cheek into his hand. When I open my eyes he is staring at me with longing in his eyes.

"I can't believe you've been watching me. I don't remember seeing you before today."

"You didn't. There's CCTV all over the building. We all have access to the one at the main entrance and everyone has access to the one on their own floor. I have access to them all, I own the building so security is my responsibility. When I first saw you, I remember thinking how beautiful you looked but also how troubled your expression was. I thought you were either there for the dentist and were scared, or you had dodgy accounts that Donald was sorting for you. When I saw you pass our offices and continue on upstairs, I knew it had to be something else. I never got up the courage to speak to you but oh how I wanted to hear your voice and look into your eyes. I watched you and over time I saw hope gradually replace the haunted expression. Then today when I called you 'Missy' that look came back and it killed me to think that I had made you feel like that. I couldn't even look at you. I thought I had blown any chance I had of speaking to you."

I turn my head away, this is a lot to take in. When I turn back to look at Steven, he is leaning in close to me. His skin is cleanly shaven and flawless, I really want to touch him. His dark hair is perfect, a bit like David Beckham's, mmm very nice indeed. I would really like to run my fingers through it and mess it up. I squirm slightly. I am so turned on just looking at him. I think if he touches me again, I will explode.

"Are you okay Gina?" His voice is soft and soothing, I could melt.

"I'm fine," I manage to whisper just as he leans in and places the softest of kisses on my lips. Fireworks blast in my ears, the sensation is amazing, I can't move. The kiss ends but, keeping his face close to mine, our noses almost touching, Steven looks right into my eyes. We sit there looking at each other for what seems like an eternity. His deep dark ocean blue eyes crashing in to my sky-blue ones. I know this is crazy and I have only just met this man but right now I would do anything he asked of me.

"Kiss me Gina," he breathes.

Ok here goes nothing. I kiss him back and this time I put in some effort. His lips are so soft. His tongue starts probing, his right hand softly perched on my left cheek. It is strange having another man kiss me this way. Aiden and I had been together for 10 years. I had been intimate with other guys at University but when you are with someone for so long it becomes familiar and routine for want of a better word. I feel Steven's left hand move from my arm round to my chest, my nipples stand to attention. He slips his hand inside the top of my dress and grazes my right nipple with his fingers. The sensation that shoots through my torso right down to my groin is intense. I wriggle a little trying to relieve the pressure but that only intensifies the feeling. Steven tears his lips from mine and my eyes shoot open.

"Take off your dress Gina." His voice is silken and smooth. I can see he is also visibly affected as I catch a glimpse of his impressive bulge. I think the wine is giving me uncharacteristic courage because I immediately stand up and undo the ties at the side of my dress. Thank God I decided on the wrap over dress and nice undies today.

"Stop" He moves my hands from the sides of my dress. "On second thoughts I want to unwrap this present."

His smile is bewitching. Loosening the inside ties he slowly opens my dress. His sharp intake of breath when he looks at what he has unwrapped gives me goose bumps.

"Fuck, Gina, you look amazing."

His words are whispered. He pulls me close and whispers in my ear:

"I am going to have you Gina and I want you wearing these when I do," he breathes as he snaps the top of my stocking. His other hand glides inside the back of my dress and pulls me into him. Oh God he is so hard.

I am about to melt into oblivion when he suddenly pushes me away.

"Someone's coming, quick into the bathroom."

I stop still and hear the creaking of the stairs, oh great I can't have my mum or dad finding us like this. I turn on my heel and dive into the bathroom. As I am closing the door, I glance at Steven sitting back on the bed at ease like nothing has happened. I, myself, look like a harlot, all flushed and breathing heavily. He throws me a sly wink and bites his bottom lip, Oh…My…God. I close the bathroom door and lean against it, sinking to the floor like a pile of wet washing just as there is a knock at the bedroom door.

"Come in," Steven shouts.

"Hi Steven." Oh shit, it's dad.

"Just making sure Gina got you everything you need. Where is she by the way? Carla wants her opinion on some dresses for the Winter Ball next month."

"She's sorting out the bathroom Martin." Steven has raised his voice slightly, as if I can't hear him. "I think she's just preening herself to be honest."

He laughs loudly at his own joke and I feel my cheeks burn. I quickly sort out my dress and tidy myself up. As I am about to leave a very wicked and un-Gina-like thought crosses my mind. I am seriously turned on and I think my rationale has gone out the window. I quickly slip out of my lace panties and hang them on the hook behind the door grinning like a fool. Oh my God I feel so brave, this could easily backfire.

When I open the door the two of them are sitting on the bed looking at some paperwork.

"Hi darling, your mother needs your expert fashion eye. She's looking at dresses for the Winter Ball and says I'm no good. What do I know about fashion? You better go and help her before she ends up with something hideous and blames me for it."

"Okay dad, don't want you getting into trouble now do we?" I smile at him.

"Steven everything you need is in the bathroom. If I don't see you before bedtime sleep well."

I flash him my biggest smile, turn and saunter out the door. I am smiling too much but I don't care. As I close the door a huge feeling of liberation washes over me. Yes, I can do things like that, I can be sexy and have fun. I just wish I could be there to see the look on his face when he finds my knickers hanging on his door.

CHAPTER 5

CLICK. CLICK. CLICK. WHERE is that noise coming from? *Click. Click. Click.* Oh for goodness sake I am trying to sleep. I am looking out the window. The garden is covered in snow. Steven is running around naked singing. My dad is going to go mental. *Click.* He is throwing stones at my window. I am here can't you see me? Oh good grief he is doing snow angels now. He will freeze. This is hilarious. The loud laugh that comes from deep inside me wakes me up and I realise that I was dreaming.

I sit up and try to focus. The room has that lovely glow that tells me there is still snow outside. My head is a little fuzzy from too much wine. Mum and I stayed up chatting into the early hours, long after dad and Steven had gone to bed. It was so good to be back home with mum and dad, not rattling around in my house all by myself. Between us we managed to pick an outfit for mum for the Winter Ball. It is a benefit dinner for underprivileged kids that is held four times a year, one for each season; mum and dad are big contributors. I have only been to one and that was just before I finished University. Aiden and I kept to ourselves mostly, social functions always seemed awkward for him. So when mum asked if I would like to go to this one, I was a bit reluctant to accept. However, I now have only three weeks to find something special to wear.

I grab my phone from the bedside table and check the time, 04:49, oh come on! I had hoped that since I was inebriated last night, I might sleep a little longer. My throat is dry, and I feel the hangover kicking in now that I am fully awake. I put my feet on the floor and shakily stand up. I pull on the robe from the bottom of my bed. My head is spinning, and I can feel the horrible watery taste in my mouth. I know right there and then if I don't make it to the bathroom quickly, I will be sporting eau de vomit at the breakfast table. I make it and slide to my knees as the retching begins. I am trying to be quiet, but it is impossible. My stomach contents have vacated yet I am still retching, yeuch! I can feel the cold sweats start, oh God, I will not drink like that again. When I am sure that I can stand I get up and head downstairs to the kitchen to find some painkillers. I try to be as quiet as possible and almost make it without a sound. That is until Clio hears me and starts an almighty barrage against the kitchen door, yelping like a dog possessed. I swear if she was mine, I would have that trained right out of her, mum lets her away with murder.

I squeeze in through the door and shush her as best I can by grabbing some chicken from the fridge and force-feeding it to her. She happily accepts my offering, has a sniff at my foot then a lick and settles back down in her basket. Now I can get on with the business of sorting out my headache, which is a million times worse thanks to Clio. Mum has a well-stocked medicine box in the cupboard. I grab two ibuprofen and a glass of cold water and head into the family room at the back of the house. I down the pills and flick on the TV. The super bright blue/white glow engulfs the room and hurts my tender eyes and I squint as I look at the screen. The massive faux fur throw on the back of the couch is a huge comfort on this chilly morning. Wrapping myself up in it I flick through the channels. Most of them are teleshopping. They make me laugh at the amount of crap they try to sell. The one with the insane workouts on it does catch my eye, though only for the fact that I really think I should use the gym membership that costs me £90 a month. I haven't been since just before Aiden died and I have had no inclination to care since. I give my belly a slap and make a conscious decision to get back to it, jelly belly is not a good look. I had to try my hardest to hold it all in when Steven semi undressed me last night. The more I think about that and how I left my knickers in his bathroom, the more uneasy I become. I must have looked callous like I didn't care about Aiden at all.

All this brain activity is hurting my head; I need something to watch that doesn't take any brainpower. I settle on the comedy movie channel, I could do with a laugh. Gross out comedy is the best for inane laughs and I see that Bridesmaids started 10 minutes ago. That will do. I am having a little chuckle to myself at a dress fitting gone awry when I get the feeling someone is standing in close proximity. I turn my head and find Steven standing behind the couch smiling at me.

"Hey Little Miss Giggles," he says with a grin and a tip of his head. He is dressed in his suit trousers and shirt but has a more casual look about him this morning with his sleeves rolled up and the top button undone.

"Hey yourself. What are you doing up at this time

in the morning? Did I wake you?"

"Not you my alarm. I don't tend to sleep a great deal but somehow I couldn't sleep much at all after finding these," he says reaching into his pocket and holding out my knickers on his index finger. I feel the heat rise from under my robe right up to my face and I imagine I am glowing more than the TV now. I know even in the semi darkness he will sense my embarrassment and I realise that I am naked under my robe. I pull the throw round me a little tighter and hope against hope that he is on his way out so I don't have to sit and squirm under his gaze for long. Of course, he plonks himself down beside me, eyeing the throw and my wide-eyed expression. He puts the knickers down beside me and I grab them, stuffing them in the robe pocket.

"What you watching?" He nods at the TV.

"Bridesmaids. I had to find something not too taxing on the brain this morning. Think I over did it last night with the wine."

My emotions are all over the place. I don't know what to do. In the cold light of day I don't know if I am strong enough to start something new yet.

"Steven, I..."

"Sshh," he says and holds a finger up to my lips.

"I want to say something, and I need you to hear me out, understand?"

61

I nod my head slightly and he slowly takes his finger away, lingering on my bottom lip long enough to create a spark in my skin.

"I know this has been a mental 24 hours for you Gina. I know that last night was the first time in over a month that you've even been at your parent's house and I feel like my being here ruined that for you. Don't get me wrong, I had the best time in as long as I can remember, but I feel like I barged in on something very personal and private to you. This wasn't how I wanted things to go between us."

"Steven please don't feel..." His finger is on my lips again.

"Let me finish Gina, please." The pleading in his eyes and his voice shuts me up.

"I want to do this right. I know there is an attraction between us, we can't deny that. I want the chance to start over again and do this the way it should have been done."

He takes hold of my hand and presses a gentle kiss on my knuckles, closing his eyes. I feel a spark again and a warm feeling drifts out over my skin from where his lips have been. He lets go and stands up and I suddenly feel very cold.

"I am leaving now Gina, whatever happens from here on in is up to you. I think you have to realise that there are a lot of people around you who care a great deal. You might think that you can deal with grief on your own, but you can't, no one can. Believe me, it will only get worse if you don't do something about it and the more you push people away the less likely it will be that they will stick around. Whether you want to admit it to yourself or not, you need your friends and family and they need you. I personally think you are being very selfish. You're worried that people will see you as weak if you ask for help. That's not how it works Gina. You have more than enough help, so use it and stop pitying yourself."

Who the hell does he think he is? I can't believe he would speak to me like this; my life is no one else's business but mine.

He closes his eyes and a frown forms on his forehead. It's as though he is fighting some internal battle with himself. "You know where my office is, I'm there most days and some nights. I have to know that you want the same thing as me and I don't want you to feel pressured in to anything that you or I would regret."

His expression is solemn, and I can't help but feel there is more to this. I think back over last night and wrack my brain trying to work out how he knew I hadn't seen my parents in so long. It hits me...dad. They were talking for ages after I went to help mum. God only knows what he told Steven. Obviously his opinion of me has changed. He is looking at me with pity not the hot, lustful look he had last night. I have become the pathetic widow who almost jumped into bed with the first guy who showed any interest. His words sting more than I would like to admit and I can feel my blood start to boil.

"Do you think I'm a fucking moron Steven?" The words stream out of my mouth as if I'm possessed. I can't stop.

"Do you think I would have let things get so far if I was fragile and couldn't think for myself?" I am almost screeching now, and I know I will be heard if I carry on like this. "Just go Steven, I really couldn't give a shit. You don't know me, and I don't need your pity."

He is staring at me, his eyes wide and bright and the fucker is smiling. What is it with him? Is he really trying to piss me off? Yes, the ball is in my court now and I am not taking this anymore.

"Go to fuck Steven. Don't hang around waiting for me, I don't need this shit. I have enough on my plate and I don't have the energy to deal with your fucking mind games."

Tears are threatening and I wish he would leave. I was trying to be strong and show everyone that I can handle things on my own and yet again my towering strength has been demolished by people always thinking they know what's best for me. I think I am more enraged by the fact that Steven does actually seem to know me better than I know myself. Maybe I have been selfish. Why could I not have figured this all out on my own? Why did it take a stranger to get me to realise what I was doing to myself and everyone around me?

"I will be waiting for you Gina, even if it takes you months to realise what you want, I will wait, and you will come to me." And at that he turns and walks out the door.

"Fuck it!" I scream at his retreating back as the tears come rolling down my cheeks. I don't think I'm shouting at him though.

As soon as I hear the door close, I wrap myself up in the throw and sob. Everything Steven said makes perfect sense. It bloody hurts but it's true. I am crying for the life I have lost. Everything that made me who I am was ripped away from me and I don't think I have grieved properly for myself. Yes, I cried for Aiden and how he would never get to accomplish everything he wanted but I never once gave a thought to my own life. It was destroyed along with him and I have been living in a state of limbo for the last six months. My eyes feel so heavy and I feel my bones and muscles ache. It seems as though all the hopelessness I have been carrying around is seeping out in my tears and my body is becoming a puddled mess. My sobs are loud and echo in the big quiet house, but I don't care. My eyes close and I feel myself drift off to sleep, the tears still flowing, and playing in my mind are the last words I ever said to Aiden.

CHAPTER 6

"CLIO SHHH." I HEAR my dad chastise the dog.

"Carla will you come and get her she's going to wake Gina?"

"It's okay dad I'm awake," I say in a very raspy voice. I don't know what time it is or how long I have been asleep, but my eyes feel like they have their own airbags and my neck and throat hurt like hell.

"Are you okay my darling?" His voice is soothing and reassuring. When I look at him his eyes are sad, and he has an air of guilt about him. "Gina I'm sorry. I feel like this is all my fault, I never meant for you to feel like this."

I feel terrible for him. I now realise that I have put everyone through hell for the last six months while I was wallowing in self-pity. I had the help, but I chose to ignore it. It felt like people were interfering not trying to help. I reach out and take his hand and he comes and sits beside me and wraps me in a big warm daddy hug. Even in my thirties I still love my daddy like I was a little girl and I know that he would do anything for me. I feel him shake a little and realise that he is crying. My big strong father is crying, grieving, and it's all my fault.

"Oh dad I'm so sorry for shutting you out, please don't cry."

In that very moment I realise that I wasn't the only one who lost someone dear. My mum and dad doted on Aiden; he was like their surrogate son since they only had me. But more than losing him they lost me. They lost their little girl. I can't begin to imagine the pain they must have felt. I did that to them and I need to put it right.

"I know you spoke to Steven about me and I'm grateful to you. I needed to be put in my place and I now know that people are not pitying me because Aiden died, they are pitying me because I did. I was stupid to think that I could handle this on my own. I didn't even listen to the one person who was really there to help me. Nate is very good at his job, but I think I've given him a run for his money. Please believe me dad, things will change."

"Oh darling, I didn't say much to Steven about you. Really, the only thing I said was that I was so glad you had come to see your mum and I, since we hadn't seen you in over a month and that I thought you two had hit it off."

I smile at that. 'If only you knew he was stalking me daddy'.

"He's a good judge of character and being a stranger probably meant that he didn't treat you like a wee doll that could break like we all did. I think we were holding you back as much as you were."

His eyes have dried, and I can see his strength return

"Did I wake you and mum? I'm sorry for the shouting and most of all the swearing."

I rarely swear in front of my parents and I feel a little disrespectful at the way I screeched at Steven in their home.

"No, actually, I was woken by the phone. Steven called to talk about the project we're working on and he asked me to make sure you were okay. He didn't go into details and I won't ask what went on, it's none of my business, but I will say he is a good lad. I respect him immensely. He didn't have the best start in life, but he has made a bloody good name for himself."

My dad respects him? He must be a good guy.

"Thanks dad, I love you and mum so much." I snuggle in and hug him tightly.

"We've missed you my darling," he whispers into my hair and kisses me lightly on top of my head.

"I missed you too daddy," I say with a smile.

I must have slept for well over two hours after Steven left, and after my heart to heart with dad I feel more human than I have done in months. I have showered and dressed. Since I didn't plan on visiting, I had no change of clothes and have borrowed a pair of jogging trousers and a t-shirt from mum.

Sitting in the kitchen having a coffee mum asks: "Are you okay honey?"

"Honestly mum I am better than I've been in ages. I feel like I know what I need to do to get my life back. I'm so sorry to you and dad for what you have been through because of me."

I look at her and her face is flushed, her eyes glassy as if she is going to cry. I can't do another round of tears, I'm all cried out.

"Mum please don't cry, I think my tear ducts have shrivelled up."

She snorts out a laugh. "Oh honey we were so worried about you for so long and I was wondering what the hell the point was in therapy if it wasn't helping you. I'm glad things are looking up, but you do know that it's not an overnight fix, don't you?"

"Yes, I know that mum, I'm just seeing things much clearer now. I'm going to give Nate a call and find out if he can see me today. I need to get everything off my chest. I think now that I know which direction I want to take with my life his job will be a lot easier."

Poor Nate, I know how wonderful he is at his job and I talked a load of bullshit to him trying to make out that I was in a better place than I actually was. I have a lot of making up to do and today is my clean slate.

"That's good darling, I'm so pleased. Would you like some breakfast? I have croissants, or you can have some toast or a bowl of cereal?" Her voice sounds calmer, but her eyes deceive her. I can still see hurt behind them, hurt because of me.

"Toast will do fine mum."

As soon as she rustles the bread packet Clio is at her ankles yipping away. I laugh at her as she spins around her ankles like helicopter blades while mum nearly breaks her back trying to avoid standing on her.

"Mum I think you'll need therapy because of her shortly."

I am laughing now and feel a sense of wellbeing wash over me. I notice the sun is shining outside and go to the window to have a look out. Most of the snow has melted and I turn to mum with a look of confusion. She gives a little chuckle.

"Oh honey when dad and I got up this morning it was pouring with rain and most of the snow was gone. You were so sound asleep I don't think world war three would have woken you."

"It was a whiteout last night as well."

At that moment I remember what Steven said; 'Do you believe in meant to be?' Maybe the snow was meant to be, maybe Steven being here was meant to be and maybe all of this was meant to be to save me from myself.

"Mum I'm going to head home in an hour or so, I really have a lot to be getting on with."

"Dad will drive you home honey. You can get a ride in the new 'wheels'." I laugh out loud at her air quoting my dad. "He's trying to be hip with the youngsters."

"Thanks mum. I love you."

CHAPTER 7

THANKS FOR THE LIFT dad," I say as he pulls into my driveway.

"Anytime sweetheart, don't be a stranger okay? Mum and I always love to see you."

"I won't dad, I love you"

I lean over and kiss him on the cheek and get out of the car. He blows me a kiss and I hold out my hand to catch it and slap it on my cheek. He laughs as he drives away. As I walk to my front door my heart is heavy. I have decided, in my current state of enlightenment that this house is not what I need anymore. It is one of the many things holding me back. I mope around in here all day and every single bit of it reminds me of Aiden and makes me sad. At my parent's house I felt hope, but I could sense the fog returning as dad rounded the corner into my street. This house, our 'wee nest', is just an empty shell to me now. If I am to make a fresh start, I need to do it right, I need to clear out my whole life and start again.

The air inside is as cold as it is outside, and I shiver as I close the door. I turn on the heating to try and take the November chill out of the air and head for the kitchen to make myself a coffee. With the kettle on to boil I fish my phone out of my bag and call Nate's office. The line rings twice then I am greeted by:

"Dr Dempsey's office, Fiona Speaking. How may I help you?"

I love Fiona's voice; it is so bright and cheery. She is not pretentious or fake; she is a genuinely nice person.

"Hi Fiona, it's Gina Connor."

"Gina, hi. Is something wrong? We don't normally see or hear from you from one week to the next." She has genuine concern in her voice and it is heartening to know that someone, who is in essence a stranger to me, cares.

"Don't worry Fiona I'm perfectly fine. I was just wondering if Nate could squeeze me in sometime today. I need to speak to him about something and I would prefer to do it sooner rather than later."

"Oh Gina I'm sorry his day is absolutely full. Can you give me a minute, is it okay to put you on hold for a sec?"

"Of course Fiona, please don't put him out though I can wait if need be."

"Won't be a mo."

The line clicks over to the mechanical hold music. From my limited knowledge of classical music I recognise this as 'Moonlight Sonata'. I remember trying to play this on a keyboard in my music class at high school, albeit very slowly and without any chords. I smile and close my eyes. My mind flits to Steven, remembering the music he had on in his car, and just like that Beethoven is gone and Fiona is back.

"Hey Gina, sorry to have kept you there. Nate says if you can make it in for five pm, he will see you after hours, and before you say anything, we are off out to dinner in town after work so you're not putting us out."

"Thank you Fiona, you're a star. See you at five then."

"See you later Gina."

I hang up and check the time. It's just after midday so I have a few hours before I need to leave. I am happy that I have stuck to my guns and am finally facing my fears, but I am filled with a sense of foreboding. I am going to the building Steven owns, the building where Steven has access to all the CCTV cameras. He will know I am there, but I don't think I am ready to see him yet. It bothers me slightly that within 12 hours of meeting me he knew so much about me. What also bothers me is the effect he has on my senses. No one, not even Aiden, has ever had that effect on me and it is causing my mind and body to war with each other. I give myself a mental shake. 'Que sera sera' as Doris would say, what will be will be and there is nothing I can do about it.

Forgetting the coffee I decide on a nice glass of wine and a long warm shower. The quick five-minute shower I had at my parents' house this morning didn't quite cut it and I am expecting birds to start nesting in my hair. The house is starting to warm up and the steam coming from the shower is glorious. Flicking on some music I get undressed and step under the warm spray. As I stand there, water running over my face, my mind drifts to Aiden. What would he think of me right now? He would probably be laughing at me, I am sure of it. I'm not sure he would have had this problem if he were left behind. Would he find it easy to move on?

Hair washed and body scrubbed I feel much better. I dry off and moisturise then pull a satin slip from the wardrobe and put it on. I like the cool feel of it against my skin. It makes me feel sexy, a feeling I don't experience too often these days. I can't stop thinking about Steven; he made me feel sexy last night just by the way he looked at me. I really wish it hadn't ended the way it did. I feel terrible for the way I spoke to him this morning; all he was trying to do was help. I am about to leave my bedroom when the photo I have on my bedside table of Aiden and I on our wedding day catches my eye. We are standing outside the registry office looking into each other's eyes. I feel the tear falling and before I can wipe it away it drips from my cheek on to the glass between us. We will never be together again, and nothing can change that. I lift the picture and kiss his face. It's now or never. If I don't end this vicious cycle I will never move on.

"I am so sorry Aiden," I whisper and hold the frame over my heart. "I will always love you."

I pull the attic steps down and climb up, God if anyone was behind me, they would be getting an eyeful. It makes me laugh and I think of Goldie Hawn in 'Bird on a Wire' the only difference being I don't have Mel Gibson's face in my ass. Just at the top to the right of the opening is my memory box full of Aiden's things that I kept; the rest went in the bin or to the charity shop. Boy that was an experience. My mum, Aiden's mum and his sister helped me. I would have kept the lot and made my house in to a shrine if it hadn't been for them. The box contains our first movie tickets, our first dinner receipt, our wedding paraphernalia, and silly photos, simple things that always make me smile. I have a little search around and find what I am looking for right at the bottom. The walnut ring box is still polished and shiny. I take a deep breath and open it. Inside is one solitary platinum ring. Aiden's wedding ring, one of the few things I got back from the police in a clear zippy bag with his name on it. I rub my thumb over the precious metal. It is stone cold. I place the box on the floor and remove my engagement and wedding rings. I tuck them inside the box next to Aiden's ring. There they all sit cushioned in cream faux leather. I lift the box and place a lingering kiss on all three rings.

"Goodbye my love."

To my surprise I am not crying. I touch my lips and realise I am smiling. I put the ring box back followed by the photo, still in its frame. As I replace the lid a feeling of liberation washes over me. I finally feel at peace, as though those last two things were holding me back.

CHAPTER 8

THE BUS GETS ME into the City Centre by 4.30pm and it is already dark. I decide to get off at Buchanan Street bus station and walk the rest of the way. It is not raining or snowing, and the air is crisp and cold. What a difference a day makes. The Christmas lights are twinkling in shop windows and overhead. It is closing time for a lot of the offices and rush hour is well on its way. There are shoppers and commuters everywhere and the streets are buzzing. With only four weeks till Christmas the shops are open later than usual. When I am finished with my meeting, I decide to catch up on some Christmas shopping.

The walk up Sauchiehall Street, through Charing Cross, takes around fifteen minutes and as I turn the corner onto Royal Terrace, I feel a knot tighten in my stomach. I know Steven is still in his office because his car is parked right outside the building. I walk up the stairs to the front door with the knowledge that Steven can see me. I hope he sticks to his word and lets me deal with this in my own time. I am not ready to see him yet. I make it to the third floor undisturbed and as I open the door to Nate's reception area, I am greeted with Fiona's smiling face.

"Hi Gina," she beams. "He is just finishing up his last appointment, take a wee seat."

"Thanks Fiona. So where are you two off to tonight? Special occasion?"

"Nate is taking me to the Grill on The Corner then off to the cinema. A wee date night since the girls are over at mum and dads for a few days before they go off on their cruise."

She always has a twinkle in her eye when she talks about her and Nate's three-year-old twins. Two beautiful blonde girls whose photo has pride of place on their parent's desks.

"Sounds fab, I love the Grill on The Corner, their steaks are lovely."

Just as she is about to answer I hear Nate's door open. He bids farewell to his client then turns to me.

"In you come Gina." He beckons me in to his room.

"Right Fi get your glad rags on."

She gives a little giggle and he winks at her. They are so sweet together it makes my heart hurt to watch them. I walk in and take my usual seat.

"Thanks for seeing me Nate I know your time is precious, so I won't take up too much of it, especially when you don't get much time to yourselves. It must feel good to get out without the kids, but I bet you miss them when they're not around. They must be getting big now eh?"

Oh God, I am rambling like an idiot, just like my mother. When I look at Nate, he is sitting back in his chair with his fingers steepled in front of his mouth, his legs crossed, and his notebook balanced on one knee. He is smiling, and I instantly feel the heat rise up my neck and my cheeks flush.

Lowering his hands he says: "Finished?"

I nod, too embarrassed to speak.

"Good, good. First of all, I have been waiting for this moment for the last five months Gina. You called to see me. This is a big step and I know that something significant has happened since I saw you yesterday. Secondly, our reservation isn't until seven thirty and we are leaving from here, so I am giving you a full hour. Just start from the beginning and we will take it from there okay?"

Instantly at ease I tell him everything from the

moment I was told Aiden had died to my heart to heart with my dad this morning and my decision to sell the house. It feels good to finally be telling someone about this and with every word the fog around me begins to lift. The only information I omit is anything about Steven. Obviously, they know each other considering this is Steven's building and Nate rents these offices from him. For all I know they are best mates. I don't want my personal life being discussed over a pint down the pub. '*Oh get a fucking grip Gina, he's your doctor*'. When I glance at the clock, I am amazed to see that I have been talking nonstop for over twenty-five minutes. It is already a quarter to six. After a few moments of silence Nate says:

"So you thought that this therapy was a waste of time? You thought if you bullshitted me and told me what I needed to hear that it would all be over quickly, and you could be done with it? I knew you were lying right from the start Gina, just like I know you are not telling me the whole truth now."

I bow my head in defeat. How could I have ever thought Nate wouldn't see through me? He is brilliant at his job. I know I need to tell him, but I can't seem to find the words.

I sit in silence trying to avoid his gaze. He waits. It's now or never, I know he won't let up. "I...met someone...here...yesterday when I left..." I can feel the tears threatening behind my eyes.

Sensing my unease Nate says: "Okay, I can see this is hard for you so let's play a game of 'Guess Who'. Just nod or shake your head to answer, okay? You tell me as much as you want. Yes?"

I nod in agreement.

"Okay. Question one, was this person a male?"

Nod.

"Very good. Question two, was this person known to you before yesterday?"

Shake.

"Three, are you attracted to him?"

I can't answer. It's as though my neck bones are fused together. Nate's voice becomes softer.

"Three, are you attracted to him?"

I don't know what to do. As I slowly nod my head, I feel the hot tears rush to the surface, spilling over the edge. I know these are tears for the life I have lost. It is true; I have never fully grieved for myself. I was too concerned with the fact that Aiden had lost his life, but I never gave a thought to the fact that a massive part of my life ended that night as well. Now that I think there may be a chance for me to start over again and be happy it feels wrong.

"Let it out Gina, this is long overdue." He reaches over and hands me a box of tissues.

"Grief is a funny thing you know. There is no set way for you to feel or deal with your emotions. Everyone's 'revelation' comes at a different time. Sometimes I can be seeing someone for over a year before it hits them. Yours has come quickly by most standards. I could have sat here and told you that I knew you were lying but that wouldn't have made you acknowledge the problem. I had to wait until you were ready to let me in and we finally got there. I don't care who this guy is, but it is obvious to me that meeting him has changed your outlook on life and that can only be a good thing."

I am a total snivelling wreck now and he sits quietly for the longest time until the tears go, and I am no longer sobbing.

"Remember Gina, this is not over by a long shot. You still have a long way to go and you have to keep your friends and family close. You will have good days and bad days and after a while the good will outweigh the bad, but don't run too far on those bad days. You need to stay strong."

His words are reassuring, and I feel a million times better. He looks at the clock above the ornamental fireplace and says, "Are you going to be okay or do you want to call someone to come and take you home?"

My gaze follows his and I see that it is well after

six pm. I realise that this is his way of saying *'Come in Gina your time's up'*.

"Oh Nate I'm so sorry, I'll get going. I've taken up more of your time than was necessary."

"This is my job Gina and if a little after-hours work is needed then so be it."

His smile is warm and comforting and I know that I have done the right thing by coming to see him today.

"I don't know how to thank you," I say as I stand up and offer my hand. Instead of reciprocating he pulls me into a hug. I am slightly shocked by this.

"Just remember I am here if you need me, Fiona too," he says as he releases me.

"Thank you again Nate that means a lot to me." I turn and pick up my coat and bag. "Enjoy your night out."

"Oh, we will, don't you worry."

I say goodnight to Fiona, apologising to her for monopolising her husband. With a parting wave I tell her she looks lovely.

Making my way downstairs I feel a renewed sense of purpose. The next few days will be critical to getting my life back again. As I pass Steven's door I stop momentarily and consider knocking. With a shake of my head I realise that I need more time. I head down the last flight of stairs and out into the cold night with my head finally held high.

CHAPTER 9

THURSDAY MORNING CONSISTED OF many phone calls and note taking. My first call was to mum to tell her all about my meeting with Nate. I didn't mention Steven. That can wait until I am sure there is something to tell. I also told her about my intention to sell the house. She was very supportive and said she would help me out as much as she could.

I called my friend Charlotte or Charlie, as she prefers to be called. We have been best friends ever since we started Uni together. Originally from South Africa Charlie came to Scotland to study Zoology at Glasgow University. She was one of the lucky ones who left with a degree and got a job that was worthy of it. She started out in animal welfare at Edinburgh

Zoo and now works as a press officer for the Royal Zoological Society of Scotland. We got chatting during fresher's week while we were both signing up for the tennis club and hit it off. We remained close after graduation and she was chief bridesmaid at my wedding. She is yet another person that I have shunned lately, and she was over the moon to hear from me. We arranged to meet up for lunch on Saturday in Glasgow City Centre. We have so much to catch up on.

My last calls of the day were to the estate agent and my solicitor. Aiden and I had decent enough life insurance policies for £100,000 each plus a policy that would clear the mortgage if either of us died. Our little house on the outskirts of Glasgow is only worth £110,000 but it is too much for me to continue paying for on my own. The fact that the mortgage was paid off after Aiden's death helps a lot. The life insurance was paid out quite quickly and has kept me going financially for the last five months.

What I hadn't expected, a month after Aiden's funeral, was to find out that he had taken out a separate life insurance policy that he hadn't told me about. The first I knew about it was when I was clearing out a filing box of Aiden's with a load of letters and paperwork in it. Why hadn't he told me? It turned out Aiden had taken the policy out at the beginning of the year. He used a different solicitor to the one we had already and there was also paperwork relating to a will. We had never discussed making wills before. I wish he had told me. I hated thinking he was hiding things from me. Half a million pounds is a lot to hide from your wife. Absolutely every piece of correspondence in the box was addressed to Aiden's mum's house. It left me with more questions than answers. I used to think he was the other half of me, that we knew everything there was to know about each other. But there have been a few other niggling little things that have come to light since he died that have had me questioning how well I actually knew my husband or if I even knew him at all.

What was even stranger was that he hadn't named me as the beneficiary. He hadn't named anybody. I was his wife so automatically became the beneficiary. I had it transferred to my solicitor, but I haven't been able to touch it. Mum and dad both said that obviously Aiden wanted me to be looked after but all I felt was betrayal. Mr Mitchell, our solicitor and mum's old colleague, was very happy to hear from me. I made an appointment for Friday afternoon; I have a surveyor coming in the morning to value the house. With my plans in motion I felt a sense of relief that everything was okay and no catastrophic event had occurred.

After dinner, which consisted of a scrawny baked potato and some cheese that was teetering on the edge of extinction, I decide to do a little research. Google has always been my go-to and today it will help me find a new place to live. I think I will try finding somewhere in the City Centre. I have always wanted to be surrounded by lights, noise and people. After searching a few estate agency websites I find a couple of flats that take my fancy and bookmark the pages as my mind wanders to Steven. I have resisted the urge over the last couple of days to Google him...until now that is. I am curious. If he is the big hotshot businessman mum and dad claim he is then there is bound to be something interesting to read about him.

My cursor hovers over the search box. No, I can't, that's an invasion of his privacy. *'Yes and he was watching you on CCTV cameras for months'*. Okay then...a search it is. I type in his name. It takes me a few seconds to press the enter button and I close my eyes as I do. The pages that come up are newspaper articles and a few blog type posts by celebrity spotters. Celebrity spotters? Now that has piqued my interest. There is also a Wikipedia page. Jesus, he has a Wikipedia page. Who the fuck is this guy? Before I read any of those I click on the tab for images. The first few are pictures of Steven at what looks like dinners or functions of some kind. He looks very dapper in his lovely tailored, very expensive suits. God he is so gorgeous, just looking at these pictures is making my belly flip. My eye is drawn to a picture a little further down the page and I feel a knot tighten in my chest. The woman in the picture is so beautiful with her immaculate blonde hair, gorgeous makeup and absolutely stunning figure. She is holding Steven's arm like a vice and they are looking into each other's eyes and smiling. The feeling of jealousy that rips through me is so intense it frightens me a little.

Slamming the laptop shut I get up and pace the floor of my little kitchen, but my eyes are drawn back to the table and the laptop. *'Oh for goodness sake Gina give yourself a shake. You only met him two days ago, isn't he allowed to have a life before he met you?'* I return to the table and open the laptop again. The screen flashes back to life. I decide to look at the Wikipedia page. This should be interesting.

There are only a few paragraphs of information with a couple of links dotted here and there. The first paragraph is a general blurb about him and his career. He graduated from Glasgow University at 24 with an honours degree in Civil Engineering with Architecture. He designed a building in Madrid and had it built by the time he was 26 and, it appears, he has had a hand in a few other rather famous buildings around the world. He is quoted as saying his biggest influence in his working life was his engineering lecturer who took him under his wing and gave him the confidence to become very successful. OH MY GOD! My dad has a mention on Wikipedia. This is surreal.

"My career would be nothing if not for the perseverance and positive influence of my favourite lecturer Martin Harper. He is a wonderfully intelligent man to whom I owe my livelihood and life," Steven is quoted as saying.

I sit back staring at the words on the screen in front of me. He owes his life to my father? My head is starting to ache. I think this is the most stimulation my brain has had in months. Flicking back to the images. I click on the link for the one with him and his lady friend. It is from an article in The Scottish Sun. The headline reads:

'The Names Blonde, Double Oh Blonde.'

Obviously referencing the fact that she has platinum blonde hair and he looks like James Bond. I hate stupid tabloid puns. I glance at the date on the article and am more than a little shocked to see that it is from this morning's edition of the online paper. This picture was taken yesterday? What the fuck? He left me in a state yesterday morning and went straight out with this bimbo! I am seething. More at myself for being so stupid. Of course he would be out with beautiful women, he is stunning, what the hell would he actually want with me? I am a failure at everything. My degree got me jack shit and my business has more or less failed. What the hell do I have to offer someone who already has it all?

'By Tracie Evans. Published 15 hrs ago

'Glasgow's big business was out in force on Wednesday for the Young Entrepreneur awards at the city's Hilton Hotel.'

There's a blurb in the middle about who won what and all the other business people who were there. I scan down a little further and read on.

'Among the guests was millionaire property developer, architect and former Young Engineer of the Year award winner Steven Parker. Pictured above with his stunning date, he was presenting the award which launched him onto the world engineering and architectural stage. We do not know who his mystery date was, however, they remained close throughout the evening and reports suggest that Steven is currently unattached, making him one very eligible bachelor. Maybe this is the beauty who will finally steal his heart.'

I feel sick to my stomach. What was I thinking; changing my life because I thought there was something worth changing it for? Do I really want to be part of that life anyway? It all seems a little too intrusive. I didn't realise how well known Steven was or how rich he was, and it's all a little disconcerting. I shut down the laptop with a sigh. I think a little wine and music may help my mood. This is ridiculous, who on earth decides to upend their whole life for a man they just met and know nothing about? No, I am changing for myself. I need to make this break, or my life will stay as shit as this forever. I have to believe I am worth more than this.

I pour myself a glass of chilled Pinot Grigio from the fridge. Other than some milk, butter, cheese, and wine my fridge is bare. I don't know what I have been living on if I am really honest with myself. I take my wine and some breadsticks I found while rummaging in one of the cupboards and decide on an action movie for the night. Although these were Aiden's favourite films I do enjoy a good action movie and right now I want nothing more than to watch things being blown up. I haven't been able to watch any of these DVD's because they reminded me too much of Aiden. Wow, there really has been a shift in my psyche. This is a big turning point for me and it feels good. As I settle down to watch 'Die Hard' my worries over my past, present and future melt away under gunfire and explosions for a while. 'Yippie ki yay motherfucker!'

CHAPTER 10

IT'S SATURDAY AND I have made my way into Glasgow to meet up with Charlie. Being the end of November it is St Andrews Day soon and everything is adorned with Scotland flags. We chose to meet at the little coffee shop on the top floor of Princes Square. We used to come here all the time when we were at Uni, although this wasn't a coffee shop then, it was a bridal shop. We would sit in the Chinese restaurant next door and talk about our dream weddings and husbands. I miss those carefree days.

When I arrive at the coffee shop, Charlie is not there yet so I order a latte and take a seat. I am sitting rummaging through my bag looking for my phone when I hear the unmistakable lilt of Charlie's voice.

And God have I missed it.

"Gina my lovely."

I turn and see her gorgeous smiling face and my eyes are immediately drawn to her belly. She is wearing a tight-fitting V-neck top and a pair of skinny jeans under a lovely big chunky knit cardigan. Her long blonde curls frame her glowing complexion. Oh my God, either she had a big breakfast, or she really does have a lot to tell me. She looks absolutely gorgeous. I stand and hug her and immediately my eyes well up. I can't let go of her and put my head on her shoulder.

"Oh Charlie I'm so sorry." I manage to squeak out.

"Come on darling don't you go getting upset, I'm very emotionally unstable right now and you'll set me off."

I give a little laugh at that; we both know she is the most stable person on the planet. In all the time I have known Charlie the only times I have seen her cry was at my wedding and Aiden's funeral.

"Let's sit down. I need a strong coffee since normally I'm 'not allowed'." She air quotes that last bit with a roll of her eyes.

"I'll go and get you one, you..."

"No...watch this," she laughs and proceeds to shout over to a young guy wearing a black uniform who is clearing one of the tables.

"Hi there babe, would you be a doll and bring me a latte? This baby is getting restless and my feet are absolutely killing me," she coos, batting her eyelashes at the poor unsuspecting boy. That, coupled with the lovely tones of her South African / Scottish accent, makes him look like he may kneel at her feet.

"Of course I can. Is there anything else I can get you?" His little cheeks have gone a lovely shade of pink.

"A bit of that lovely carrot cake would be great, thanks." She winks at him and I roll my eyes at her and smile. God, I have missed her.

"Coming right up," he beams.

When he is out of earshot, I look at her smiling face. "You are bad Charlie."

"Well, why not use getting fat to your advantage. You seriously would be amazed at what people will do for a pregnant woman."

A few minutes later the poor sap delivers the coffee and cake to our table and she thanks him with a little kiss on the cheek. He stands there for a few seconds with his hand over the place she kissed then walks away in a daze. I give a little laugh and then ask while pointing at her bump. "So this is rather big news Charlie. Will you please fill me in?"

We sit there for over an hour as she tells me about

her own last six months. Turns out that she met a guy called Mark at work around three months before Aiden died. She had told me about him when she first met him, but they had only gone on one date by then and I never really thought to ask her how things had gone. She actually found out she was pregnant a few weeks after Aiden's funeral. Every time she tried to tell me she just couldn't, she thought I would hate her for being happy. I completely shut her out over the last five months, those precious months when she probably needed a friend more than ever. I feel terrible, but she doesn't resent me, she should but she doesn't.

"Gina you were dealing with a massive loss, I couldn't bear the thought of me making it worse. I did call a few times, but I thought it was best to let you get on with things in your own time. I knew you would get in touch when you were ready. When you called me the other day, I was so excited, I just knew that I had to see you in person to tell you about this," she says as she motions to her bump.

"So, how far along are you then?"

"Six months. I only have about twelve weeks left. I didn't know how Mark was going to take it and I didn't tell him for about four weeks after I found out. Of course, he was over the moon, which floored me I have to say. I was expecting to be bringing this baby up on my own. We'd only been seeing each other for about three months and there was so much we didn't know about each other. I've fallen for him though and I really think for the first time in my life I am truly content and happy. When I told mum she squealed down the phone. I don't think I needed a line to Joburg. If I stood outside, I could probably have heard her. She's making plans for her and my little sis Nikki to come over when the baby is born."

I love this girl. She always has found the positive in everything. Her mantra is 'everything happens for a reason' and I am starting to think she may be right.

"So Gina, don't think you are getting away with not telling me what's been going on with you. I know something has happened. When I spoke to you, I knew something had changed, so spill biatch." She is giggling like a fool.

Being my best friend gives her access-all-areas to my personal life. We always shared everything about everything with each other, so I tell all. When I am done, she sits back in her chair with her hands clasped over her belly and a massive smile on her face.

"So what are you going to do about him then? Are you going to see him again?"

"I don't think so, that picture in the paper more or less made my mind up. His life is too different from mine. I don't think I would fit in to it."

"Stop talking shit Gina, you know as well as I do that you like him, I can tell by the way your eyes light up when you speak about him. Come on babe, it's time you got on with your life and even if it doesn't work out with him it could be fun in the meantime, he sounds dishy. I might just have to look him up myself." She winks one of her gorgeous green eyes at me and I smile.

"He is more than dishy Charlie, he's like something that fell out of GQ." I feel myself blush. "I don't know what to do yet, I think in all honesty I'm scared."

"Well I'm gonna help you honey. Let's have some retail therapy, and then I want to go over to the Uni. I miss that place, we can grab lunch over at Byers Road and then go for a wee stroll in the park."

The way she says 'wee' in her funky accent melts my heart. This has been good for me and I vow we will never lose touch again. I am going to make sure I spend more time with her and be there for her when this baby comes.

We leave Princes Square just after midday and exit on to Buchanan Street where the streets are filled with Christmas shoppers. It's almost December and there is a definite festive feeling in Glasgow. We head to Frasers where we spend the next hour trying on designer clothes and scoring each other as if we are at a beauty contest. I don't think I have laughed so much in ages and it feels great. I buy a lovely navy-blue dress, which feels like it could have been made especially for me. It fits like a glove and looks beautiful with the nude heels I chose to accompany it. Who knows I may just get to wear it. I also decide to get my dress for the winter ball, it's a beautiful plum coloured maxi dress with little diamanté embellishments at the waist and is daringly backless. This is not my normal get up, but it makes me feel good and Charlie's wolf whistle gives me the push to buy it.

Leaving Frasers we head for the Subway station at the top of Buchanan Street. This takes me back to being a student. I used to get the subway every morning over to Byres Road, which takes you out almost at the University's front door. The subway station has had a bit of a makeover, but it still has that distinctive underground smell. As we sit and wait on our train I look over at Charlie.

"What?" She says as she cocks her head at me.

"I love you to bits Charlie you know that, I'm so happy for you," I place my hand on her belly and I feel her little baby moving.

She smiles at me and whispers: "She likes you."

I stare at her in a mix of confusion and shock. "You know?"

"Yes, we found out a month ago. I have been hoping since then that you would get in touch so that I could ask you this. Before I found out I already had names in mind for a boy but only one for a girl. I want to call her Georgina."

I am so taken aback that I feel my eyes start to flood. This is ridiculous, I stop myself before I start bubbling again.

"Oh Charlie, I would be honoured to have her named after me. Thank you."

"No…thank you Gina. This is great I can get other shit done now that is out the way, phew."

She laughs as she swipes her hand across her forehead. As the train pulls in to the station I am filled with happiness. I have my parents back and I have my best friend back. Just one thing left. I will work on that later, for now I am going to enjoy Charlie.

CHAPTER 11

AFTER LUNCH AT ORAN Mor, a beautiful restaurant and performing arts venue in an old renovated church, we walk past the University on University Avenue. This is one of my favourite places. The old buildings were built in a Gothic Revival Style and are located on the hill overlooking Kelvingrove Park. Charlie and I, and a few of our friends, used to go down to the park when the weather was nice and have picnics. I use the term picnics very loosely. Mostly it was fish and chips and a few bottles of beer. Those were the days... when we didn't have a care in the world, when all we cared about was making lectures and what pub we were going to that night.

"God Gina, this place brings back memories," sighs Charlie as she looks up at the buildings from across the street on Kelvin Way.

"Oh, I know honey, how often do you just wish life could be that simple again?

"Hey, do you remember the time Ritchie Michaels streaked at the book club's summer barbeque down at the park? I actually thought if you could die laughing that would have been the day to do it. Do you think they ever got over it?"

Charlie snorts and within seconds the tears are streaming down her face. "Oh my God Gina I think I peed my pants a little, come on this is not fair."

She is holding onto my jacket sleeve and crossing her legs. "Remember the look on Professor Paton's face? I thought she was going to combust she went so red. Bet it was the first real life cock she'd ever seen. I'm surprised she never put it on a finger roll and called it a hot dog."

We are both laughing our heads off when Charlie suddenly stops, eyes staring, mouth almost on the pavement. I follow her gaze. Sitting next to the kerb is a now familiar sight. A lovely sleek Aston Martin. Oh God how am I going to handle this? The window slides down and there sits Steven in all his gorgeousness.

"Hi Gina, how are you?"

I don't know what to say or do. I look across at Charlie who mouths 'he's gorgeous' to me with a knowing wink. I feel my legs shake a little and my heart rate is steadily going up.

"Can I give you girls a lift anywhere?" His voice is lovely, but it has an edge to it today.

"I could use a lift to Queen Street Station if you're going that way? My feet are bloody killing me and this little one thinks my bladder is a punch bag today."

I flash Charlie a 'what the hell are you doing' look.

"No problem at all..." He pauses and looks over at me…waiting.

"This is my friend Charlie, Charlie this is..."

"Steven," Charlie says. "I've heard all about you."

She gives a mock innocent smile and a little wink. I want the ground to swallow me whole right now. My cheeks are burning even though it is freezing outside.

"Oh really," Steven says as he gets out of the car. "All good things I hope."

His smile is unbelievably sexy, and I am finding it hard to hold onto my composure. I can feel myself melting under his gaze. He is dressed in a pair of faded jeans and a V-neck jumper. He looks unbelievably laid back and sexy.

"Oh yes very good things." The bitch is giggling now. *I am going to throttle you Charlie*, I think with a smile.

"Gina, how about you, where are you going this afternoon?" He looks at me with those deep blue eyes, the corners of his lips curled in a delicious smile. I can't deny it, the attraction between us is electric and I am finding it hard to resist pushing Charlie over and running right into his arms.

Instead I nod and say: "I'm going to Central Station. Going to see mum and dad."

I chastise myself inwardly, too much information Gina.

"Okay I'll take you both to your stations." He has a mischievous little smile on his face and I am slightly apprehensive about where this afternoon may go. But I also think this may be a good chance to find out more about the mystery woman.

"Ooh...I've always wanted a ride in one of these." Squeals Charlie as she tries to climb into the back seat.

"Don't think so Charlie." Steven shakes his head.

"You might fit but that bump won't. I'm sure Gina won't mind a wee ride in the back seat for now, eh Gina?"

The innuendo in his words is palpable and obviously not only to me, Charlie is smiling like a

107

lunatic. I give a little sigh and a nod and climb in. He wasn't kidding about the seats; it's like being in a sardine can. Innuendo or not, no 'ride' will ever happen in here. Charlie carefully manoeuvres herself into the front seat, which is so low I fear she may have trouble getting back out. As Steven pulls away from the kerb, I am aware of him glancing at me every now and again in the rear-view mirror. I feign indifference not wanting him to see how he affects me. He flicks on the stereo system and we are greeted with a blast of 'Blurred Lines'. Really? I didn't think he'd be into this. As Robin Thicke drolls out 'I know you want it' Steven catches my eye in the mirror and gives me the sexiest wink I have ever seen. I am aware of a tingling sensation in my knickers and abruptly break eye contact.

Before I know it, we arrive at Queen Street Station and Charlie is excited about the gaggle of curious onlookers who have gathered to look at the car.

"Hey, look it's my adoring public," she laughs.

Steven gets out and walks around the car to help her out. Humouring her he opens her door and says: "Here we are ma'am, no pap's here, if you hurry into the station no one will notice."

Charlie giggles. He grabs her bags and hands them to her. I notice a few of the people have their phones out ready to take pictures, obviously thinking someone famous must be in the car, won't they be shocked when they get Charlie. Just then a sinking feeling comes over me. Steven is, by all intents and purposes, famous in his own right. These people will now have pictures of him. Pictures of Steven and Charlie together. I wonder just how long it will take for these to appear in the paper and what the pun will be this time. Steven pulls the seat forward and I get out of the car and kiss Charlie goodbye telling her to text me as soon as she gets home.

"I will doll face and thanks for today, I had fun. We'll be seeing more of each other now yeah? Don't you go shutting down again, baby Georgie needs her auntie Gina around." Her gorgeous smiley eyes make me feel happy inside. I really have missed her.

"Of course we will. I am never letting you go again Charlie Barley."

We hug each other tight and off she goes.

The crowd has dispersed now, however, I notice a man standing by the stairs next to the entrance doors. He is a big guy and looks very unkempt. He's staring at Steven and his look is full of loathing. I catch his eye and he grins at me with an ugly, partially toothed mouth. I have to look away, he is creeping me out. When I turn back to the stairs he is gone. I shiver. Is this what it would be like being with Steven? Always being watched. I never actually thought about that side of being so well known. There are some seriously fucked up people in this world and all it takes is one.

"Ready Gina?" Steven's voice breaks through my chilling thoughts.

"I can walk from here Steven. Thanks for dropping Charlie off, I'll be fine."

As I bend to get my bags from the car, he grabs my wrist. "Gina don't be silly. I'll take you to your mum and dad's. I was just on my way home so it's not going to take me too far out of my way."

His smile is melting me, but I need more time. "No, honestly Steven, I already bought my ticket and the train takes me almost to their door."

My fake smile is unconvincing and when I look at him his eyes flash with a look that makes me feel uncomfortable and turned on at the same time.

"Get in the car Gina."

When I hesitate, he raises his voice very slightly. "NOW."

Oh! The authoritative tone in his voice takes me by surprise and I am so shocked I do as I am told. This was not the Steven who spent the night at my parent's home. This is a different person altogether and, strangely, I think I like this one better. When I am seated, he closes the door and slides in to the

110

driver's seat with ease.

We sit in silence as we make our way round George Square and head towards my parents' house. We have been driving for about five minutes when Steven says: "So what have you been up to since I last saw you?"

I know he is asking if I have sorted my shit out, but I want to know what he's been up to and who with.

"I could ask you the same thing," I say keeping my gaze on the road ahead. I am surprised when he answers without hesitation.

"Mostly working and I had an awards ceremony on Wednesday night. I go to it every year because I won one of the awards when I was younger and this year, I got to present it. So I'll ask again, what have you been up to?"

There is that voice of authority again. When I don't answer him he asks: "Have I done something wrong Gina?"

"Who was the girl 'double oh seven'?" I blurt out. My voice sounds snarky and not like me at all. I look over to him. He is staring straight ahead and doesn't speak for ages. As I am starting to think I have overstepped the mark he looks at me and smiles.

"Are you jealous Gina?"

"No," I say a little too quickly and look down at

my hands.

"Gina, as I remember from our conversation on Wednesday morning I was told to 'go to fuck' and that you didn't 'need this shit'. I wasn't actually planning on seeing you this quickly after I was lambasted by you. I said I would be waiting for you, I did not say that I would put my life on hold. So tell me, how does it have anything to do with you what I do in my own time?"

When I look at him his expression is cold. I shiver at the thought that I may have completely and utterly ruined this.

"I'm sorry." I feel like I have just been punched in the gut and my eyes fill with tears that I know I won't be able to stop. This seems to be all I have done for the last five days.

I am so wrapped up in my own little world of misery I don't notice that we are not en-route to my parents' house. I know this place. This is just around the corner from Steven's office building. This is Claremont Terrace.

"What are we doing here?"

He doesn't answer, he simply gets out of the car and comes around to open my door and holds out his hand for me. I hesitate, searching his face for clues. Why has he brought me here? Still holding my hand he leads me up to the front of a beautiful sandstone building with columns on either side of the door. It is similar to those on Royal Terrace but much more refined. We walk to the front communal entrance and Steven pulls a set of keys from his pocket. Oh my God is this his house? I gasp as we walk through the door.

CHAPTER 12

"STEVEN," I WHISPER, OVERWHELMED by the sight of the entrance hallway.

He looks down at me, his face expressionless. I think I really have pissed him off this time. We take the stairs and enter the apartment through a massive black door. Inside I am confronted by the most stunning hallway I have ever seen. The floors are tiled in a creamy coloured quartz, which sparkles under the LED lights. Immediately ahead is an elegant black baby grand piano and next to it sits a shiny silver saxophone on a stand. I wonder if he plays them or if they are just for show. To the left is a massive room with double glass doors. Inside there is a large snooker table at one end, which looks like it probably cost more than my house, with a large sofa at the other facing an impressive wall mounted flat screen TV. Silently Steven leads me through the glass doors to the right. It is furnished with two large cream sofas facing each other over a marble coffee table. This will be the lounge then. We carry on through to the kitchen, which is just as stunning as the rest of the apartment, before Steven let's go of my hand.

"Drink?" There is not a glimmer of a smile and I am feeling a little apprehensive.

"Water will do fine thanks."

He takes a bottle from the fridge and says: "Give me your phone."

"What?"

"Give me your phone."

"Eh…I don't think so." I am a little annoyed by the way he is acting. Why does he want my phone?

"Why? Surely you have one of your own." Two can play at this game pal.

"I have several, but I want yours."

"Tell me why you want it first," I say with a cocky smile holding it up, just out of his reach.

"You're not going to win here Gina so just give me the phone."

I am starting to get mad. Who the hell does he think he is trying to order me around like that I am not about to hand over my personal property to someone I hardly even know. *'Yes and you are in his apartment with him and you hardly even know him.'* As I stand there warring with myself, he blindsides me by slapping the underside of my hand sending the phone into the air. He catches it in the same hand, the whole movement so fluid it's as if he has practiced it a million times. I'm so shocked I laugh. That could have gone spectacularly wrong. It has a pass code so I'm not worried. I don't want to make this too easy for him. As I stand there with a smirk on my face, I see him start messing about on the screen. I think he has managed to unlock my phone!

"What the fuck Steven! Have you unlocked my phone?"

"What if I did?" He says with an evil grin on his face as he hands it back to me. I look to see what he has been doing and almost immediately get a text from mum.

'That's okay honey we will see you on Monday. Are we still okay to come over for dinner?'

Above mum's message I see one that I didn't write.

'Hi mum I can't make it over tonight, I'm staying at a friend's house. Love you. X'

No way. He did not just text my mother for me. I

116

could have done that myself. And staying the night, I don't think so pal.

I text mum back.

'Yes mum Tuesday is fine, sorry about tonight. X'

"What are you all about Steven? Do you think I am incapable of texting my own mum? And how the hell did you get into my phone anyway? You're very sure of yourself, aren't you? Who says I would stay the night? I'm not ha..."

My voice is swallowed up mid-sentence as Steven grabs me and fits his mouth over mine. Oh my God his lips are divine. We keep our eyes open and fixed on each other. This is bloody hot. When we eventually unlock lips I try to sound as angry as I can.

"What the hell are you doing? I'm trying to be mad at you."

He is smiling at me and I can't help but smile back.

"Gina, your dad once told me that sometimes the only way he knew to get your mum to shut up was to kiss her. I was just trying out his theory."

"My dad told you that? Steven just how friendly are you and my dad?"

I am very curious. I know nothing about this man, yet he seems very familiar with my family. My dad has a bloody mention on Wikipedia because of him for God's sake.

"Your dad is my hero Gina. I love him like the family I never really had, and I owe him an awful lot."

As he looks away from me, he picks up an empty envelope from the worktop and starts playing with it. He looks nervous.

"What do you mean you owe him? What happened to you Steven?" I try to keep my voice as reassuring as I can, but I feel tremors in every word.

He remains silent for the longest time and then as if a switch has been flicked, he puts the envelope down and walks to the fridge.

"Would you like a glass of wine?" He says calmly ignoring my questions. I decide to let it go for now. Wine sounds good to me.

"Yes please."

He takes a bottle of rosé from the fridge and I watch as he uncorks it. The way his muscled forearms flex as he turns the corkscrew and opens the bottle is so sexy. He fills a wine glass and hands it to me. He opens a slim cupboard, which by the looks of it houses all kinds of spirits and mixers, and takes out a bottle of whisky. The amber liquid is like fire as he pours it into a glass and seems to stick to the sides like honey. Steven lifts his glass in salute.

"Slanj-uh-vah, gorgeous." He gives me a wink

and tip of his head and takes a sip from the glass.

Mesmerised, I watch him as he swallows the whisky; the muscles in his throat contract and he closes his eyes, savouring the taste. I am lost. He is absolutely perfect. His face is symmetrical and flawless, his hair thick and glossy and the one-day stubble on his jaw line perfectly complements the casual look he has going on today. God, he makes even the simple action of drinking look incredibly sexy. I wish I were that whisky running down his throat, warming him from the inside.

Eventually becoming aware of myself again I find I am copying his movements, swallowing my wine and closing my eyes. My free hand is on my neck and I can feel my own throat muscles flexing. An unexpected feeling of fearlessness overcomes me as I rest my hand on my clavicle. Fully aware that he will, by now, have opened his eyes and will see everything I am doing I move my hand lower still, until it rests on the swell of my breasts over my t-shirt. I hear his sharp intake of breath and the knowledge that I am turning him on is intoxicating. I lean back against the worktop and tilt my head back slightly. I have never been so brazen in front of anyone before, not even my husband, and it is a liberating experience. I allow my hand to slip inside my top and run over the satin and lace of my bra. I move my fingers inside the cup of

119

my bra and run my index finger over the hard nipple beneath. I am so turned on now that I couldn't stop even if I wanted to. Removing my hand, I open my eyes and look over to where Steven is standing. He is staring at me, the corners of his mouth curled in a sexy semi smile. I smile back and dip a finger from my free hand into the cold pink liquid held in my other hand. I put it in my mouth and suck long and hard on it all the while watching as Steven's expression changes from amusement to fascination.

I can see from the strain in his jeans that his body is responding ardently. Spurred on by his obvious arousal I take a large drink of my wine then open the button on my jeans and lower the zip revealing the top of my lace knickers. Feeling slightly self-conscious I close my eyes and slip into a fantasy world. My hand disappears in behind the lace brushing over the coarse, damp hair there. I am so aroused that I know if I hit the right spot just once it will send me over the edge. I let my hand linger a moment listening to Steven's breathing become more ragged. I am completely at the mercy of my own hand and it has been so long since I have had any sexual pleasure that the need to let go is acute. I think about Steven watching me pleasure myself and as I do my finger slides just beneath my folds and skims my clitoris. It is hot and swollen and aching to expel the

120

pent-up tension. That one tiny touch sets off a chain reaction and as I slip a finger into the hot wetness and rest my palm over my mound my body lets go. I feel my muscles contracting again and again. I am thankful I am leaning against the worktop otherwise I might collapse.

Before I can regain my composure, I am caught by a strong hand on my lower back and another behind my head. Steven's lips are on mine in a hard and desperate kiss, his tongue trying to force its way into my mouth. I oblige and taste the warming whisky in his mouth.

"Oh my fucking God Gina," He says, his lips still on mine. He pulls away far enough for me to see the desire in his eyes. He pushes his hips against mine and I can feel his erection and, oh my goodness, it feels impressive.

"Can you feel how hard you've made me? That was fucking unbelievably sexy."

I smile and before I can say anything his mouth is on mine again, this time a little softer than before. An image of Aiden flashes into my mind. He is standing in his biker leathers with his arm hooked through the helmet giving me a thumbs up with a smile on his face. I feel a tear escape and Steven feels it too. He stops and pulls back to look at me.

"Gina, what's up?" His voice is full of concern.

I can't answer. What do I tell him? In the middle of the most erotic foreplay I have ever had, with the most gorgeous man I've ever had, I was thinking about my dead husband. I shake my head and pull him towards me. He responds, and his kiss is more forceful this time. His hand moves down from my back and cups my behind, giving it a tight squeeze. I feel like my body is on fire, every single nerve ending is lit. With my arms round his neck, he lifts me up onto the worktop with ease. He bites my lower lip until it is just on the verge of painful. I reach up and feel it is slightly swollen. A tiny bit harder and he would have drawn blood.

He trails hot wet kisses from my neck to my shoulder pulling my top to one side so that his mouth can stay connected to my skin. The long-sleeved T-shirt I am wearing has buttons half way down and he undoes the first two exposing the top of my breasts. His kisses continue, and he bites ever so slightly at the soft flesh. This sensation is exquisite. Another two buttons and the top is open to just below my bra. His kisses advance further down to my cleavage and the feel of his hot breath on my cool skin sends shivers through me. My nipples are as hard as stone and begging to be touched. He releases my breasts as the last button is undone.

Steven takes his lips from my skin and trails a

finger across my exposed breasts, I am absolutely spellbound. Abruptly, he lowers his hands to the top of my jeans and gives a tug. Automatically I lift myself on both hands just enough for him to pull them down. He slides them down over my knees, planting soft little kisses on my inner thighs as he goes. He quickly discards most of my lower garments on the floor and looks at me

My sex is absolutely soaked, and I fear that if he doesn't fuck me soon, I will slide right off the worktop. Steven eases my breasts out of the cups of my bra pushing them upwards.

"Mmmmmmm, fucking gorgeous tits Gina."

He takes a sip of whisky and, holding the drink in his mouth, encloses his lips over one of my rock-hard nipples. I feel the liquid slide over my skin as his tongue swirls in circles, round and round, so many sensations… my brain can't keep up. Steven swallows the whisky and keeping my nipple in his mouth sucks hard on it, pulling it deep into his mouth. He pulls back releasing my breast and blows on my wet nipple causing it to erupt like a volcano. A shudder tears through me and I feel as though I am about to rip apart. I try to focus, I don't want to be spent by the time he gets into my knickers. He has one hand on my back and the other is splayed on my belly as he gently pushes me back. I let my head fall back and close my eyes. His hand moves down and cups my sex over my knickers.

"You're soaked Gina, my God you are so ready."

"Oh God…yes…Steven, please," I manage to whimper. If he doesn't do this soon, I will expire.

As I balance on my elbows Steven pulls my hips to the edge of the worktop. I look down as he undoes his jeans and I can see his hard-on straining through his underwear. He is, by all accounts, still fully clothed while I am almost naked save for a few bits of skimpy material.

"Take off your t-shirt," I more or less demand.

He smiles a wickedly sexy smile and grabs the hem of his t-shirt pulling it up and over his head. My gaze travels from the gorgeously toned muscles below his navel, up over his perfectly ripped abs. He has the most beautifully sculpted body I have ever seen. There is a scattering of hair on his chest, which trails all the way down disappearing beneath his boxers. Oh, how I want to follow it and see what the prize at the end is. His arms and shoulders are something else.

"Nice guns." I am momentarily shocked by the words coming out of my mouth. I did not mean to say that out loud. He laughs at my horrified expression. This is rapidly replaced by shock as Steven unleashes his hard-on. It's bloody massive. He moves closer and pulls me up, so my bare breasts are pressed against his chest. He grabs my head at the back, pulling slightly on my hair.

"You like what you see Gina?"

He whispers in my ear. His hot breath is stoking the flames of my desire for him.

"I'm going to fuck you hard and you're going to love it. You're going to come like you never have before. And I'll be right there with you."

Oh my good God, I'm about to fall apart just from the sound of his voice? He brings his head to face me and seals his mouth over mine.

I can't take the anticipation any more.

"Yes Steven, I want you to." My voice is raspy and my throat dry. He responds by pulling my knickers to the side and slipping a finger into my drenched pussy.

"Oh, fuck this I can't wait any longer, I need to be inside you."

He reaches into his jeans pocket and pulls out a condom. He sheaths himself so quickly I barely register it. Then he is probing at my entrance. The thick head prying for a way in. The passage is smooth as I am positively dripping wet for him, but it is still a tight fit. As he slips his tip inside me, he groans, a most raw and primitive sound, and it makes me clench my muscles around him. I swear he could make me come just like this.

"Fuck, Gina."

I raise my hips slightly so that he can get deeper. When he is in to the hilt, he flexes his dick and the tip presses on a sweet spot deep inside me. He starts to move backwards and forwards. Small movements at first then building to a steady rhythm. I move my hips to meet his thrusts and it is not long before we are in sync, our bodies welded together. With each upward thrust he strokes my swollen bud. I feel myself at the precipice of a long-awaited climax and with one hard thrust and slight twist of his hips Steven takes me there and I feel as though it might rip me in two.

"Oh God, oh my God, Steven."

My words are barely audible. As the muscles deep inside me flex, I dig my nails into his back and hold on for dear life. My body is a shuddering wreck and I feel his body quiver as he let's go and fills me with his hot and heady release.

"Jesus Gina, you've fucking ruined me," he growls leaning his head on my chest. We are both damp with sweat and breathing rapidly and it feels fantastic. When we both come back down to earth, he looks into my eyes and mouths the words 'thank you'. Slowly pulling out of me he discards the condom and lifts me off the worktop. He carries me out of the kitchen and all I can do is hold on. I am spent, my eyes are heavy, and I feel the need to sleep hit me like a freight train.

CHAPTER 13

UPSTAIRS IN THE MASTER bedroom Steven places me on the enormous wooden bed. A sheet of gossamer fabric is threaded through four large brass rings at the top of bed posts and are draped down either end skimming the floor with a swag in the middle. The sheets are cream Egyptian cotton. I can feel that they are very expensive and luxurious under my bare legs. Steven walks into the bathroom and starts to run a bath. A flowery scent wafts from the bathroom. Closing my eyes, I let the smell engulf my senses. I feel myself drifting but am brought back to the present when Steven runs his hand up the inside of my leg. Opening my eyes I find him sitting on the bed smiling down at me. His jeans are open at the fly.

He looks unbelievably sexy and I feel like pinching myself to make sure this is real.

He reaches out and strokes my hair. "You okay babe?"

All I can do is nod my head.

"Come and have a bath with me."

He holds out his hand. My legs are a little shaky but most of all I feel exhausted. As we walk into the bathroom, he turns to me and lifts the hem of my T-shirt, pulling it over my head and throwing it into the laundry basket in the corner.

"Turn around."

He says as he twirls his finger in the air. He unhooks my bra and slides the straps over my shoulders. I feel his breath on my neck as he pulls my hair up and ties it in a messy bun. I have never had so much attention lavished on me by a man before. Steven definitely knows what he is doing. It feels rather decadent and I like it…I like it a lot.

His hands move to the elastic of my knickers and he slowly slides them down my legs and as I step out of them, they follow my top and bra into the laundry bin. I wonder if he is going to wash my clothes for me. The thought makes me smile a little. '*Of course he's not Gina you twit*'. Steven takes my hand and before leading me to the bath he plants a soft kiss on my lips. I kiss him back and lean in closer. The feel of

129

my breasts against his bare chest is sublime; the scattering of hair tickles me slightly and makes my nipples harden in response. I could stay like this forever. When he breaks the kiss, I feel deflated. He tugs on my hand and leads me to the huge oval shaped bath, keeping hold until I step in to the lovely warm milky water. As I sit down, I feel my muscles relax. The smell of roses rises up in the vapour. I wonder if this is what heaven feels like. Steven leaves the bathroom for a second and the room is plunged into complete darkness. There are no windows and the only light emanates from the bedroom. Just as I am thinking the fuse must have gone or something, I hear a click and little sparkly LED lights come on in the ceiling panel. They look like little twinkling stars in the night sky. Muted light rises up from around the skirting boards. I feel as though I have been transported in to a fairy tale when I hear music start to play. Where the hell is that coming from? It sounds similar to the piano music I heard in Steven's car the other day.

To my delight a naked Steven walks back in to the bathroom. This is the first time I have seen him completely naked and what a magnificent sight it is. His movement is fluid and confident. I am a little dumbstruck and I know I look like I am catching flies, but I can't help it. He slips in behind me, his legs on either side of mine and wrapping his arms around me pulls me back until I am lying on his chest, the warm water lapping at my belly. I swear I could live in this moment forever. The thought startles me and I open my eyes. I have never thought like that before, not even with Aiden who was the love of my life. Steven takes a washcloth from the side of the bath and runs it up my arm and round over my breasts. As I close my eyes again, I feel a tear run down my cheek. Bloody brilliant! He lifts his other hand and takes the cloth down my other arm. The cool air on my warmed wet skin gives me goose bumps and I shiver slightly. I can feel the tears flowing freely now and I daren't turn around and look at Steven. I let out a little sob, I can't help it, and my body jerks.

"Gina, what's wrong?" Steven's voice, full of concern, makes it worse and I am now in full flow crying, sobbing and sniffling. I feel his body stiffen as he sits up and pulls my arm so that I am facing him. What am I doing? This guy is perfect in every way; he is just what I need. Nate was right, I do need more therapy.

"Gina will you tell me what's wrong? Have I done something to upset you?"

"I'm sorry Steven. I don't know what to do?"

"About what? Gina please talk to me. Do you

want to get out of here?"

I nod, and he stands abruptly and steps out, grabbing a towel from the heated rail and pulling it round his waist. He pulls another bigger one off and gestures for me to stand up. He holds my hand and helps me out. I am so cold I am shivering like a leaf, even though the bathroom is warm.

The tears are still streaming down my cheeks as Steven opens up the towel and wraps me up tightly. He holds me there for the longest time as the crying subsides and I am left with little gasps every so often. When I have stopped crying and shivering, Steven unwraps me and rubs the towel over the bits of my body that are still damp. It is such an affectionate act and it feels good to have someone take care of me. I don't know what will happen when I tell him what my tears are always for, but I know I have to tell him. It's not fair to keep making him feel like shit because I can't move forward. Steven disappears into the bedroom and comes back carrying a navy-blue T-shirt and wearing a pair of light grey pyjama trousers, his torso bare and beautiful. He puts the t-shirt on the bars of the towel rail to warm it up slightly.

"Right, when I say now drop the towel and I'll put this over your head. That way you won't lose the heat from it. Okay?"

I nod.

"Ready, steady, now."

I drop the towel and he pulls the T-shirt over my head. It is lovely and warm and way too big for me. Looking down at it I see a familiar sight. I have this exact t-shirt at home, albeit in a much smaller size. It has a University of Glasgow logo on it. I smile at that. We at least have something in common. We both went to the same Uni, oh, and we both know Martin Harper.

Steven holds out his hand for mine and leads me into his bedroom and sits on the bed. I sit opposite my gaze on my legs instead of on him. This is where I will probably lose him. What man in their right mind would want to hang around with this fucked up mess of a woman? Who really wants to compete with the memory of a dead man?

"Right Gina," he says breaking into my thoughts. "Are you ready to talk?"

I open my mouth to speak but nothing comes out. I don't know where to start. He takes my hand in his and rubs my knuckles, reassuring me. It makes it a little easier.

"You basically know what happened to Aiden. I told you at my parent's house. I've been seeing Dr Dempsey since just after the accident because my own doctor said I had PTSD. I had been telling him what I thought he wanted to hear for the last five months in the hope that he would just sign me off his books and I could go back to my pitiful existence."

"Gina you're not pitif..."

"Stop Steven," I cut him off. "Please just let me speak."

"Sorry, go on."

I take a deep breath and continue. "I got into a routine with the therapy, I think having something to do every week broke up the monotony. I was kind of coming to terms with the fact that my life was fucked. Then I met you."

I look up at him and he smiles.

"The way you looked at me that morning at my parent's house made me feel pathetic. To be honest, I already knew that's how everyone looked at me. Pitying me, walking on eggshells around me, careful how they spoke in front of me. But you looking at me like that hurt. I used to let everyone else's pity wash over me but you..."

I stop for a moment, unable to find the words to describe how I felt.

"When you drove away from the bus stop that night, I realised I had probably messed up my chance to truly move on, I didn't even know your full name or anything about you. I decided then that I wasn't going to be the old lady with no family and only a wee dog to love her."

He looks puzzled.

"I'll tell you some other time. That's why I was at mum and dads that night. It was because of you. After you left me that morning, I decided I needed to speak to Nate and tell him the truth. Before I got there, I dealt with a few things."

I hold up my left hand to show him that the rings have gone. His smile is tinged with a little look of sadness. Not pity.

"I didn't tell Nate who you were, I just told him that I had met someone when I was at his office. I thought you might know each other, and I didn't think it was appropriate to spill my guts about you."

I look down at my hands as I tell him what I told Nate.

"Nate confirmed what I had already worked out that morning, that I hadn't actually dealt with the fact that when Aiden died my life just stopped. Everything I knew was gone but I only felt the loss of him, not my own life. I didn't understand that by shutting everyone out I was actually damaging myself. I can't actually believe I am going to say this to you. Please don't hate me."

I bow my head. Steven reaches up and tilts my chin so that I am looking at him.

"Gina you don't have to tell me anything if it's too hard for you. I think you've been incredibly brave telling me what you have already."

I need to get this out; I need to start to repair my life, so I continue: "Every time I feel like something is going well, I get a horrible feeling that I'm somehow being unfaithful and disrespecting Aiden's memory. Any time I am with you I find myself thinking about him. I'm sorry but he was my husband for fuck sake. I just don't know how to be happy anymore. I don't feel like I deserve it. I don't know how I can go on living my life and grow old when he can't."

A tear drops from my cheek and lands on my bare leg. Steven moves closer to me and pulls me onto his knees. He holds me tight against his chest.

"I will make you happy again baby, I promise." He murmurs into my hair. He moves us so that we are lying down in the middle of the bed, the front of his warm body pressed against my back. We stay like that until my crying stops and I feel myself drift into a dark restless sleep.

CHAPTER 14

I WAKE TO PITCH dark and silence and am momentarily disorientated. I don't know where I am, and I reach out my hand patting the bed beside me. It is empty. Oh no, no, no, no. There is no one there. I hear a strange sound like an animal in pain. It is only when I feel hands on my shoulders that I realise the sound is coming from me.

"Aiden no, where are you?"

"Gina. Gina wake up."

My eyes fly open and it takes me a moment to realise who I am looking at.

"Are you alright?" Steven says staring at me with a look of fear in his eyes, his face illuminated by the light coming from the bathroom. It is dark outside, and I have no idea how long I have been asleep or what time it is.

"Yes. Just a bad dream I think."

I am so embarrassed. I know I shouted Aiden's name and here I am semi naked in Steven's bed. What must he think of me?

"I'm sorry Steven, I'm so so sorry." I sit up and put my head in my hands. This is not fair to him. It's always going to be like this, I just know it. Everything makes me think of Aiden and I don't think I want to forget about him. If I am honest with myself, I am scared of what my future holds for me now. I had my life all planned out and now it is back to the drawing board. Steven reaches over and puts his hand on my chin with just enough pressure so that I have no choice but to raise my head and look at him. He has that little smile on his face again and my heart is breaking. I feel torn between feeling happy and feeling like I am being unfaithful.

"Gina, I told you I would make you happy again. I'm not expecting you to forget about Aiden, I would never ask that of you. He was a massive part of your life and that's what he will always be. That's what makes you the special person you are, so caring and compassionate and willing to put everyone else before yourself. Please believe me, I have enough experience to know when someone is a good person and when they are not. Compared to some you're a saint. Please let me in Gina, let me help you."

I am an absolute mess inside. My heart is screaming out yes, but my head has other ideas. "I just don't think I'm strong enough for this."

"Do you trust me Gina?"

Do I? I don't really know him well enough to make that judgement but somehow, somewhere deep down inside, I think I do. I think I believe that he can help me. This is the hardest thing I have ever done in my life and I know it is going to be an uphill struggle I just hope he doesn't let me down. I don't think my fragile heart could take it.

"Yes."

He pulls me close to him and holds me tight. "Good. I promise I will take care of you."

With that sentiment hanging in the air he wraps me up in the duvet and we lie down together. I feel myself drift off to sleep with a smile on my face. My first hopeful smile in such a long time.

***

The smell of coffee assaults my nose as I wake from the most restful sleep I can remember. I can see sunlight peeking through the blinds, it must be morning. I am so warm and cosy in this big bed that I daren't move but that smell is making my mouth water and I realise that I have not eaten since lunch yesterday.

"Morning gorgeous."

Steven's voice is like a purr and I pull myself up on my elbows to look at him. He is standing in the doorway leaning against the frame wearing a white T-shirt and faded jeans. He looks as yummy as the pastries on the bedside table next to me.

"Morning yourself." I can't take my eyes off him.

"Eat something babe you must be hungry."

"I am but I'm sorry we need to take this to the kitchen. I really have a thing about not eating in bed. I hate crumbs."

He laughs at me.

"Okay that's my first lesson, no more breakfast in bed. You get yourself sorted and I'll meet you downstairs. Your clothes are on the chair in the bathroom and there is a new toothbrush next to the sink."

He comes over to the bed and bends as if to take the mug and plate away but shocks me a little by kissing my forehead first.

"Mmmmm." I murmur and close my eyes.

"Leave the coffee, I need that."

He lifts the plate and turns to leave but not before flooring me with a sexy wink. It takes me until I finish my coffee, which I have to say is absolutely amazing, before I finally get myself out of the warmth of the bed. I make my way to the bathroom and find my clothes neatly piled on the chair. I get washed and brush my teeth and instantly feel better. When I pick up my top, a piece of tissue paper wafts out from it and floats to the floor. I pick it up and read the writing on it. 'Great Western Laundering Service'. No way! He had my clothes laundered. When did he do that? All of the layers have tissue between them and my underwear; well that's the icing on the cake. My knickers and socks are in their own little vacuum bags and are as flat as pancakes and my bra is in a little cotton zippy bag wrapped round a plastic bust. These people are good; this service must cost a fortune. I feel a little embarrassed that someone else has washed my undies, but it is nice to know that I have something clean to wear and they smell divine.

When I am dressed, I make my way down the stairs but am stopped halfway by a raised voice. I venture down a little further and hear Steven. He must be on the phone because his is the only voice I can hear. He sounds angry.

"I don't give a fuck Cerys, you know fine well I should have been informed of any developments and this is one major fucking development."

There is a pause and then he answers

"Why wasn't I told he was coming to Glasgow?

Who the hell decided that would be a good idea? Do they not know who I am or that I live here?"

His voice is incredulous, followed by another pause.

"Get some answers for me and let me know as soon as you have any news. Goodbye."

I hear the phone slam on the worktop and then he shouts 'FUCKER' so loudly that I lose my footing and let out a squeal as my bottom hits the step. Steven comes running out of the living room.

"Christ Gina are you okay?"

"I'm fine honestly, my foot just slipped. Who were you talking to I heard voices?"

"Oh just my assistant. I can't escape from work even on a Sunday." He helps me up and we walk into the living room.

"It's gorgeous outside today." He gestures to the window. "Fancy a walk in the park?"

Way to change the subject. It sounded a lot more than just work. I walk over to the window and look out. He is right, though, it is beautiful. There is a thick layer of pure white frost everywhere and the sun is shining brightly. There is not a cloud in the baby blue sky and I smile to myself. I could take this as a sign, but I think I will just enjoy it for what it is. I feel Steven come up behind me and his arms circle my waist. He moves my hair and kisses my neck as he whispers

"It's not as gorgeous as you babe."

He spins me round and plants the softest of kisses on my lips, lingering for just a second.

"Go and get your boots and jacket on. There are plenty of spare woollies in the cupboard in the hall, find something that fits."

He walks towards the kitchen as I head into the hall. I get my jacket from the coat stand and find my boots right next to it. I open the cupboard and am startled at what I see. I give a little chuckle. It is full of coats, jackets and, ski gear with a million pairs of shoes all over the place. It's like stepping into a parallel universe considering how spotless the rest of the apartment is. I find a navy woollen hat and matching gloves. They fit just nicely and are lovely and cosy. Steven walks out of the living room with two travel mugs and a paper bag.

"Take away brekkie," he says holding them up.

"That's a cute look by the way." He smiles gesturing to my ensemble. Putting the mugs and the bag down on the table Steven pulls out a blue scarf, throws it over my head and pulls me towards him.

"I like you wearing my stuff, makes me feel like you're wearing me."

He wraps the scarf around my neck, gets his own stuff on, grabs the mugs and the bag and says, "right

143

let's go."

He hands me a mug and we head out into the cold frosty morning. It is only a short walk to the park but already I can feel my nose getting cold. Kelvingrove Park is a vast sprawling green space and was my favourite place to be when I was at Uni. It dates from the 1800's and I used to sit here and daydream about aristocratic ladies from the town houses facing the park walking through here in their big dresses and parasols. We walk along the tree-lined path in a comfortable silence. I never realised I could be so at ease with someone that I don't really know all that well. I pause to sip my coffee.

"Want one?" Steven asks holding up the bag of pastries.

"Yes please, I'm so hungry."

He hands me one and I take a massive bite. The buttery pastry hits my palate and makes my mouth water. Then there are the chocolate innards. I close my eyes and savour the taste. When I open them again, he is smiling.

"What?"

"You looked like your mouth was making love to that pastry there."

He laughs a little too hard at his own joke and I turn away from him in mock disgust. As I do, I happen to glance over at the buildings outside the park.

"Hey, we're right by your office. Oh it must be great to live so close to work."

I walk over to the railings at the edge of the park to look out and am a little taken aback when I see a man standing outside the building. It is the same man from the train station yesterday. The man who was giving Steven the evil eye. He has on the same dirty clothes and looks menacing. I gasp when he looks straight at me and points to me then pulls his index finger across his neck. Good God this guy is a psycho.

"Steven!"

He is at my side in seconds, but the man has disappeared. I recount the details of what just happened and give a description of the man. I also tell him about seeing him yesterday. Steven's demeanour instantly changes. His face is like stone and there is fire in his eyes. He is seriously pissed. Without saying anything Steven grabs my hand and whisks us out of the park and back to his apartment.

"Steven will you tell me what's going on?"

My protests fall on deaf ears. When we get there, he bundles me through the front door, rather too roughly for my liking, and shouts: "Why the hell didn't you tell me about this yesterday? This cannot be happening right now. Fuck!"

He's starting to scare me a little now. I don't know what I am supposed to have done.

"What do you mean told you about this yesterday? Told you what Steven? Oh by the way there was a guy looking at you. For fuck sake Steven look at you, of course people are going to stare at you. Do you want me to tell you about every person that stares?"

I am shouting as well and am pretty pissed off myself now. "Get a grip you fucking idiot. Tell me what is going on here or I'm leaving. You know how hard this was for me to even be here with you and you are this close to ruining it."

My eyes are stinging but I have had enough tears to last a lifetime. Something is wrong here and I need to know what because it seems that, somehow, I am involved.

"I swear to God Steven I don't..."

I am cut off when he puts his mouth over mine and kisses me so deeply and passionately that I am lost for a moment. *'Thanks dad'*. When he pulls away from me, he says, "Okay I'll tell you. Can you please just give me some time? I have some things I need to sort out. I think it would be best if you go and stay at your parents for a few days. I don't think it's a good idea for you to be at home alone."

His eyes are pleading, and I think he looks scared.

"Do you know who he is Steven?"

I whisper. He nods but doesn't say anything. He turns and walks away from me taking the mugs to the kitchen. I follow and find him leaning on the worktop with his head bowed.

"Steven, please can you just tell me something, I'm scared."

He turns to me and there are tears in his eyes. Oh God this is serious and by the look on Steven's face dangerous too. "He's my dad Gina, and he's a fucking head case."

I gasp and hold my hand over my mouth. I feel myself shaking. Steven is a big guy who could probably take on the world and the fact that he is scared worries me even more.

"I will tell you but not now. Right now you need to go. Please Gina, I need to know you're safe. I need to sort this mess out. It should never have happened in the first place. I'm so sorry you had to become involved in this."

He shakes his head and pulls out his phone calling a taxi for me and giving my mum and dads address. When he's finished, he puts the phone back in his pocket and takes my hand.

"I'm sorry Gina." His voice is full of remorse as if he has done something wrong. I reach up and cup his chin.

"Tell me in your own time but please be safe and

147

keep in touch with me. What am I going to tell mum and dad about going to stay with them? This is going to be a big thing for them me staying with them twice in the same week."

"I don't think they will want an excuse Gina, just please don't say anything about this until I get it sorted."

I hear the horn of the taxi outside. I really don't want to go but he needs to sort this. I can tell it is serious, so I will give him space.

"Phone me as soon as you get there. I need to know you are safe." He pulls me close and kisses me on the forehead. "Beautiful girl." He whispers.

I step out into the bright sunlight and straight into the black cab. As the taxi pulls away, I look up at the building to see if I can catch one last glimpse of Steven, but he is not there. Sitting back in the seat I pull the scarf from round my neck and breathe in the smell. It smells just like him. Bunching it up under my head at the window I close my eyes and sob. I hope everything will be okay, but I am scared this is the last time I will ever see him.

CHAPTER 15

IT HAS BEEN TWO days since I last heard from Steven and I have been moping around mum and dad's house since I got here on Sunday afternoon. I wish I had never left him that day. Not knowing what is going on is killing me. I have texted and called him but the only time he answered was when I phoned to tell him I was at my parent's house. His answer had been short and sweet:

'That's good I'll be in touch soon.'

I remember my dad saying the other day that Steven didn't have the best life and start to wonder what happened to him? His dad looked evil and looked like he had been living rough. And where was his mother? I am going to burst if I don't find out something soon. I walk out of the kitchen and knock on the door to my dad's office.

"Come in honey." He knows it's me because mum is out, and Clio certainly can't knock on the door.

"Hey daddy, what you up to?"

"Just doing a little research, what's up sweetheart?" He says without looking up from the computer screen.

"Nothing much, I just need to ask you something about Steven."

He stops what he is doing and looks at me. All right this is my daddy, I know I can talk to him. I'm in my thirties for goodness sake, I can see who I want.

"What do you want to know?"

As brave as I am feeling I don't know how to tell him about spending the night with Steven. "You know you said the other morning about him not having the best life, what did you mean by that? What happened to him?"

He stares at me. "I don't really think it is up to me to tell you that honey. And why do you want to know about him anyway?"

He is trying hard to hide his smile, but I can see it trying to spread on his face. Oh God he knows.

"Ehm... I was just curious." I know my voice is

betraying me here.

"Yeah right Gina." His smile is broad now.

"Tell yer daddy the truth now, do you think I don't see what's going on here?"

I can feel the redness rising up my neck and before long it is all over my face. He laughs his big, hearty, daddy laugh, and I am briefly transported back to my childhood.

"Fair enough but you have to tell me as much as you know about Steven. I need to make an important decision today and I need your help."

He nods, and I tell him about my week. The only thing I don't tell him about is the gesture that horrible man made to me.

When I am finished, he sits back in his chair and smiles at me. "Oh my gorgeous girlie, I'm so happy you've found someone. Steven is a great guy, but you're right there is a lot in his past that could have swung things in the opposite direction for him."

"Tell me dad. Tell me what happened to him."

"Okay, but Gina you have to promise you won't tell him I told you this. It really should be him that tells you. I'm only doing this because you're my little girl and I want to see you happy again."

"I promise dad." I hold up my pinkie finger and he takes is with his own. "Pinkie promise."

"Steven told me some bits about his life when I

151

first met him. He was nineteen when he started at Glasgow Uni and was, if I'm honest, not the most charming student I'd ever come across. He was an arrogant little shit who didn't really care about being there at all. I think he was trying to prove something to anyone who doubted that he was cut out for University. He was clever, don't get me wrong, but he just couldn't be bothered. Something about him intrigued me though. I don't know how but I ended up being a kind of counsellor to him."

His look is contemplative and a little sad as he carries on.

"I found out after about five months that his mother died when he was a baby. She was just a young woman who'd had an affair with a married man she met while working in a pub. The guy didn't want to know about him, so she did her best with what she had. She was on her own, her parents were both dead and she had been brought up by her granny. Steven says from what he was told the granny was senile and in a nursing home by the time he was born. So, anyway, his mother was on her way home from work one night and was involved in a fight with some girls who were hanging around outside the pub. One of them pushed her out into the road. She was hit by a car and killed instantly. Poor wee soul was only seven months old, so he never really knew her. All he had were some photos and what he was told by social workers when he was old enough."

Oh my God. That poor girl and that poor little baby never knowing his mother. I can't imagine any child growing up not knowing their parents. I don't really know if I want to hear anymore

"So, obviously, because he had no other real family he was placed in foster care until they worked out what to do with him. It turned out his mother had made sure to document who his father was because she couldn't name him on the birth certificate and social work approached him. He took Steven in when he was a year old and he lived with him until he was eight years old. I don't know about those seven years in between because he never told me. But it's what happened right before he was taken away from his father that shocked me to the core."

He shakes his head and sighs. "You know Gina I could never imagine a parent being so evil to, or around, their child but this man takes the biscuit."

I am sitting staring at my dad with wide eyes as the colour drains from his face and his mood becomes sombre.

"Go on dad, I want to know."

"Okay but please remember he was only a child when this all happened. This stuff from here on is available to view on the Internet now. You know from old archived newspapers and things that have been put on there, so I am not telling you anything you couldn't find out on your own. You just wouldn't know it was about Steven."

I nod my head. I can't speak; this is a lot to take in.

"Steven's father had taken him to live in London when he was seven and was arrested and jailed when he was eight."

He stops there, and I notice his eyes fill with tears. I swallow hard and touch his arm.

"It's okay dad, you've told me enough. I think it would be best if I heard this from Steven."

"That's just it Gina, I don't think he'll tell you. He may be too worried it will scare you off. From what Steven did tell me I can gather that there was serious child neglect issues with his upbringing and with that you can be assured there was more than likely physical and mental abuse. I'm pretty sure that sort of thing would have an effect on any relationship he would try to form as an adult. That boy has been to hell and back and has seen things no child should ever see."

"Okay then tell me."

"He was arrested initially for the disappearance of a prostitute in London that was quickly upped to murder after they found her body. It was big news at the time because there was a spree of prostitute murders all over the country. You would have been about eleven at the time, just starting high school so I doubt you would remember the stories in the news. Anyway, after he was arrested, his flat was searched and that's where they found her. They also found Steven. According to the reports, he was found sitting beside her body on the living room floor."

I feel as though I am about to vomit. I cannot even bear to think of what he went through as a child. "What happened to him after that?"

"As far as I can work out, he was placed into care again. This time in London. He did tell me he was in foster care and children's homes for most of his childhood but that is all I really know. I don't know how he ended up back in the Scottish system."

The blush that was on my cheeks earlier has disappeared and I feel a horrible shiver run through me. I can't get the image of that little innocent boy left alone with a dead body. I am sickened to my core. If his dad was convicted of murder what the hell is he doing here? No wonder Steven was scared. I need to speak to him. I need to know the whole story. I feel like I may be able to help him. There is no way something like this doesn't stay with someone for the rest of their lives.

My phone buzzes in my pocket and startles me.

It's my weekly reminder that I have my appointment with Nate in two hours. Good, I can see if Steven is around and try to get some answers from him. I am really worried about him with his dad wandering around Glasgow.

"Thanks dad. I don't think any less of Steven. I'm going to go and see him after I have been to see Nate this afternoon."

"Want a lift?"

"No it's okay I'll get the train. You carry on I've kept you back long enough. I love you daddy, thanks."

"Anytime my darling, I love you too. Please take care of yourself. Will you be back today?"

"I don't know, I'll give you a call later."

I get up and give him a hug and a kiss and head out of his office. Just as I close the door my phone vibrates again. It's a text from Steven. Thank God he's got in touch.

'Hi gorgeous'

That's it! That's all I get after two days of worrying.

'Hi yourself. Where the hell have you been and why have you not been in touch before now? I was worried.'

I wait for his reply. And I wait. And I wait. Nothing. I get myself ready and head out to catch my train. I am angry but the revelation from my dad about Steven has started a chain reaction of irrational thought in my head. I make it my purpose to find out everything by the end of the day.

CHAPTER 16

AS I WALK TOWARDS Steven's office building, I have this horrible feeling that I am being watched. My mind is playing tricks on me, replaying the image of Steven's dad threatening me. Little did I know that he was a stark raving murderous lunatic! As I pass Steven's office, I resolve to look in on my way out, just to see if he's there. He never replied to my text and I am worried I may have pissed him off.

I am about to climb the stairs to Nate's office when my phone rings in my bag. I am distracted slightly by trying to find it in the mess of crap I tend to just shove in there when I hear Steven's office door open and turn to see him standing there. I want so much to run right to him, but I am annoyed at the way he is looking at me with a cocky grin on his face. It's like nothing has even happened. He flicks at his phone and mine stops ringing. I realise the cocky bastard was watching me and obviously called me as a stalling tactic.

"Oh no you don't," I say as I turn my back on him and I make it up one step before I am grabbed from behind.

He puts his large hand over my mouth gagging me and his strong arm grips round my waist. I am helpless as I am dragged backward and through the open door. He releases me only for a second before I am spun round and pressed against the door by his tall, strong body. The inside of the room is dark, and I can't see anything. The feeling of annoyance begins to subside, and I start to feel a little excited as to what might be about to happen here.

"Close your eyes and do what I say." Steven's voice is low, not quite a whisper but barely audible.

"Okay." I whisper back.

"Don't make a sound," he says in my ear as he moves my hair away from my face. I feel the goose bumps rise on my arms as his hands snake their way down my neck. I am spun around again and am now being relieved of my bag and jacket.

"You were going to try and ignore me just then Gina. That's very rude you know." His voice is gravelly and sexy as hell and I am feeling rather turned on by all this.

"Steven, what are you doing?"

"I told you to be quiet, didn't I?" he says and smacks my bum quite hard. It stings, and I am shocked at the suddenness of it. I turn around to try and see him.

"What the hell do you think you're doing?" As I ask this the stinging in my behind starts to fade to a strangely warm feeling. He flicks on a small lamp on a table next to the door. It must have the tiniest little bulb in it because it gives off very little light. It is enough, however, for me to see the wicked smile on his face. He comes really close to me now, pushing his hands into my hair and tugging my head back. His kisses on my neck leaving a heated trail.

"What do you think I am doing Gina?" His breath on my ear makes me shiver. "Do you know what you have done to me?"

He bites my earlobe hard and I let out a little squeal. This only serves to make his smile wider. "I'm going to make you scream louder than that baby. I'm going to fuck you quick and hard over that desk and you're going to beg for more. Tell me you'll beg for more."

He is still whispering and what he is saying and how he is speaking should repulse me and have me running for the hills. Strangely though it is making me feel hot and needy. I can feel my knickers getting wetter with every tug, every bite, and every naughty word. He presses his groin against me and I can feel that he is as turned on as I am.

"I have my appointment Steven I can't."

"You have twenty-five minutes, trust me babe you won't miss it."

Before I can protest, he bends down and pushes his shoulder into my pelvis lifting me off the floor. My head is upside down and I smack his bottom to try and get him to put me down.

"Steven put me down, please."

"Oh, I like it when you beg," he laughs.

"You're going to be doing more of that soon."

He puts me down facing the desk and pushes his hands hard against the seam of my jeans hitting my sweet spot immediately as I fall forward. Before I am fully aware of it, he has unbuttoned my jeans and has the zip down. He pushes his hand inside and rubs me over my knickers.

"Gina I am so fucking hard for you; can you feel what you've done to me?"

His words come out through gritted teeth as if he is trying to keep his composure while pushing his hips into my behind. I am about to crumble under him. He quickly removes his hand and yanks down my jeans, my panties going along for the ride.

"I can't wait."

Seconds later I feel the silky hot head of his gorgeous cock at my wet entrance. I hear him rummaging in his pocket for a condom and he gives me a fright when he shouts. "Fuck it!"

As he starts to pull away, I reach behind and grab his T-shirt turning myself round to face him.

"Don't, its fine Steven."

I never got around to telling him that I was on the pill the last time we had sex he just assumed that it was his responsibility.

"I know where I've been, and I trust you. It's all covered."

"Are you sure?" He stares right into my eyes and I nod. He fists his hands in my hair and gives a little tug. I close my eyes against the pleasurable pain as I am pressed over the desk again, my breasts crushed against the dark wooden surface. He smoothes his hands over my buttocks and round to my hips gripping them hard.

"Are you ready for this Gina?"

"Yes, please Steven."

I am a little shocked at the pleading in my voice, but I need him now. I have missed him, and I am working myself up into a frenzy. Just when I think he isn't going to do anything, he pushes inside me just

162

about an inch but oh my, what an inch it is. He is impressive, and my body is screaming out for more. He pulls back slightly, then with an animalistic growl he forces his way in to the hilt. The sheer size of him is beyond what I would have said I was capable of, but my body is accommodates him like a glove.

"Oh fuck Gina, this isn't going to last long."

He gets a rhythm going and I feel myself start to spiral towards an almighty orgasm. He puts one hand in front of me and rubs my throbbing clit and that is all it takes to set my nerves on fire.

"Steven." His name lingers on my lips as he thrusts home hard. My muscles clench around him as my orgasm consumes me. I feel him thicken and stiffen as he reaches climax. I can feel from the tremors in his body that this was a powerful release. He doesn't say anything as he leans forward putting some of his weight on my back, supporting the rest on his hands beside me. I don't want to move but my back and hips are starting to ache.

"Steven are you okay?"

"I'm sorry Gina." His voice is just a whisper, and then his body gives a little shudder. Oh no he's crying. What on earth am I supposed to do here? I am still lying prone on the desk and he is still inside me.

"Stand up Steven, please."

He pulls out slowly and walks away from me.

163

Gathering up my jeans and fixing myself into place, I turn to him. "What just happened here Steven?"

He is standing at the window staring at the floor. He doesn't say anything, he simply shakes his head. I go to him and put my arms round his waist from behind.

"Please Steven, did I do something wrong?" I feel his body tense under my hands and he turns abruptly.

"Don't Gina. You've done nothing wrong. I'm sorry, I just don't want to lose you after waiting a lifetime for you." He closes his eyes momentarily. "I should never have let you in." I hear him mutter to himself.

"What do you mean lose me, I'm not going anywhere." My voice is high pitched, and I can feel tears coming. His head bows again.

"Yes you are, Gina. It's too dangerous to be with me now. I can't put your life at risk just so that I can get a quick fuck now and again." He spits his words out and as if they are made of fire, they burn me to the core.

"Is that all I am to you, a quick fuck? I don't think so Steven. Tell me what is going on? You can't say things like that and expect me to just accept it and walk away."

I have fallen for him. Although we have only known each other a short time, he has helped me through an incredibly difficult period of my life. I feel safe with him. I don't think I could walk away now, not knowing what I know about him. I have to help him. My problems pale into insignificance compared to what has happened to him. He sits down in the chair behind his desk and puts his head in his hands.

"I can't tell you Gina."

"Steven, I saw the reaction you had to your father being near you. You were scared. No one should react that way to a parent. Let me help. Please Steven I can't bear to lose someone else I care about."

He looks up at me his eyes searching my face. "You care about me? You don't know anything about me Gina."

I sit down opposite him. "I know enough Steven. I've never felt this way about anyone before, not even Aiden. You've helped me come to terms with what was the worst possible time in my whole life. I thought I would never be able to be truly happy again, but you changed that. You made me realise that I had to move on. Please don't shut me out."

"You don't know what you are saying."

I am becoming increasingly pissed off with him now. I am baring my heart to him and his stubbornness to accept my help is really getting on my nerves. The similarities between us in this respect is not lost on me.

"Do you think I don't know my own mind? I've spent the last six months locked away in my own bloody head Steven. I know fine well what I am saying and how I feel. Now will you please tell me what is going on?"

"Gina I've only ever told a handful of people what happened to me and most of them were police officers when I was a wee boy. I have only ever spoken to two people in my adult life about this and even they don't know everything."

I can see tears rising in his eyes again.

"I'll tell you but only because you're part of this now and he knows you are connected to me. I need you to be safe and the only way that will happen is if you know the truth."

"Take your time." I don't know what else to say.

"I'm so sorry for getting you in to this shit Gina. I seriously thought that bastard would be locked up for life. I haven't found out what happened with that but believe me I will."

He looks down at his hands on the desk and shakes his head.

"My childhood was shit Gina seriously shit. By the time I was ten I had seen and experienced things that no child ever should. I have done a lot of therapy over the years. Nate is my therapist."

Oh God I bet he has told Nate about me. As if

reading my mind he says: "Don't worry I haven't told him about you."

I breathe a little sigh of relief and he continues.

"My mother had an affair with a guy she met one night at work. We lived on the South Side of Glasgow when I was a wee baby. She worked in the Horseshoe Bar on Drury Street on weekends. You know it right?"

I nod. Having been a student in Glasgow I had frequented that bar a lot.

"Well anyway she met him in there and started seeing him. They had an affair that lasted about three months and I was the booby prize."

The way he says this about himself makes my heart hurt for him.

"She told him about me, but he didn't want to know. She was leaving work one night when I was seven months old and got into an altercation with some drunk girls outside the pub. According to the information I have gathered, she tried to stop them harassing a wee homeless man and they set upon her. One of them pushed her and she fell into the road right in front of a taxi. She died on the scene and those girls were never caught. I don't remember her but from what I have been told she loved me very much. I spent a long time resenting my mother for leaving me. I blamed her for me ending up with that

167

fucker."

He slams his fist on the desk and startles me. "Sorry I can't do this Gina. He's already ruined my life I can't let him do it again. I just want him to fucking die and leave me alone."

A tear falls from his eye and lands on the desk. I can't bear to see him like this. I slowly rise from my seat and walk around the desk to him. When he looks up at me his eyes well up, I know how hard this must be for him. I caress his face and he leans into my hand and closes his eyes as the tears drop onto my palm. We stay like that for a while until his eyes dry. He startles me by pulling me down onto his lap and kissing me hard, trying to possess my very being. I stop him. I need him to speak to me. Assaulting my mouth like this is not the answer to all his problems.

"Steven, please. I think it would help you if you talk to me."

Abruptly his whole demeanour changes.

"You're late." He looks at his watch. "I'm sure he won't mind but you should go."

"Steven, I don't think Nate will mind if I miss an appointment. I'll go up and tell Fiona and come back down."

"I'm done talking Gina, please go to your appointment. I'll call you later."

Before I can protest any further, he hands me my

bag and jacket and ushers me out the door. "Bye."

And with that the door is closed in my face. I am furious. Childishly I give his door a hard kick and head out of the building. To hell with the appointment I am too bloody angry to speak to anyone.

CHAPTER 17

"YOU AWRIGHT THERE HEN?" The middle-aged man standing in front of me lifting the empty glasses off the table asks in a deep voice.

"I'm fine thanksh." My words are slurred and sound funny. I give a little giggle that turns into a full-blown laugh.

"Get me another one will you."

"Not a chance doll. You're too drunk. Are ye here yersel?"

"Oh yeah, here myself. Cos my fucking husband went and died on me. And him," I gesture to the front door of the pub in what I think is the right direction, "he thinks I'm just good for a quickie when he wants. Well fuck him, fuck them all, bunch of fucking bastards. I fucking hate men."

My head is spinning, and I feel like I am going to throw up.

"Right I'm getting you a taxi hen. Jesus Christ it's only bloody four in the afternoon, nae young lassie should be this drunk this early unless you're an alkie. I can tell you're no, so yer goin home. Where de ye live?"

"Fuck off you old perv, I don't need your help. I don't need anyone."

I stand on shaky legs, bumping into the table and knocking over a glass. I can feel my bravado slipping and I know any minute now I am going to start crying. I need to get out of here.

"I'm sorry." I whisper to the barman and make my exit.

As soon as I step out into the cold air, I think I am going to keel over in the middle of the street. I don't know what I am going to do or where I'm going. I am only a few streets away from Steven's place, but he is the last person I want to see me in this state. I start walking up Argyle Street. I may just go and get a hotel room somewhere and spend the night drowning my sorrows in the hotel bar. However, I find myself veering towards Steven's, as if I am being drawn to him by some unseen force. As I turn the corner on to his street I abruptly stop and back up around the corner, so no one will see me. At the bottom of the steps into Steven's apartment building stands the man himself. Beside him is the blonde bombshell from the newspaper article. She is touching his face and looking lovingly into his eyes. He never told me who she was and now I know why. They look like a beautiful couple going out for the night or returning home. There is a sleek black Bentley sitting at the kerb with the engine running

I feel myself start to cry as I lean against the railings and sink to the ground. In my inebriated state I am in no position to run away so I decide to sit there and cry. My head is fuzzy, and I can't think straight. I feel like such a fool. I have let Steven break down my barriers and get under my skin and now I feel as though he has taken advantage of my vulnerability. The ground is freezing, and I can't feel my fingers or toes.

"Yes Gina you're an idiot," I say out loud to myself. I grab the railing and haul myself up. My tears have frozen solid on my face. Just as I am about to move the Bentley drives past me and I turn my head trying to hide my face in case Steven is in it. When it is out of sight, I make my way round to the front of the apartment building. One last look before I say my goodbye to all this for good. He can keep his fucked-up life, I have enough problems of my own to deal with. When I reach the front of the building, I feel my heart pound in my chest. I want him right now, to be held by him again. He made me feel good about myself, but I hate the way I feel every time he shuts me out.

I am about to walk past the front door when my phone rings. I fish it out of my bag. It's Steven. Oh what to do? If I answer I'll be giving in but if I don't, he may never call me again. I answer.

"Hello."

"Hello Gina."

"What do you want Steven?"

"What do you want Gina?"

What the hell? He called me. "Well you called me so what do you want?"

"Ah…but you're standing outside my house. What do you want Gina?"

His voice is soft and sultry, and I am about to crumble. How does he have this effect on me? "Are you stalking me Gina?"

Oh God, how do I get myself out of this? I was sure he would be gone. I hear the front door open and look up to see Steven standing there with the phone still at his ear.

"Come here Gina." His voice is low.

"No." I try to sound defiant. All I really want to do is run into his arms. I have to hold onto the railings to steady myself.

"Please come here Gina."

Oh he's bringing out Mr Nice Guy now.

"No."

His lips form a tight line. "Last chance Gina... come here."

Fuelled by alcohol I say: "EN OH." Spelling out 'no' I laugh. He does not look amused. I hang up the phone and turn to walk away. I must have taken two or three steps before I find myself flying through the air. As I look down, I see the pavement and Steven's bare feet.

"Put me down or I will scream." As I say that he takes one of the hands from round my waist and clamps it over my mouth.

"Go on then, scream," he laughs.

When we are through the front door of the apartment, he puts me down and kicks it shut. He pushes me against the wall and presses his body against mine.

"You've been drinking Gina."

"Duh," I say rolling my eyes.

"Where have you been?"

"Not telling you."

"Okay then suit yourself. I was worried about you after you left my office you know."

He moves back from me.

"Ppfftt. I didn't leave your office Steven, you put me out."

"Yes and I'm sorry for that. I find it hard to talk about my childhood Gina. I want to tell you, believe me I do."

"Okay, fine but I need to know something first."

"What?"

"Who is she Steven?"

His expression does not falter. "Who?"

"You know who. The blonde who was in the paper with you and who I just saw you with here."

"Oh, her." He is smiling that cheeky smile that normally makes me melt only right now it is getting on my last nerve.

"Yes who is she? Is she your girlfriend, your wife, your hooker? What?"

He throws his head back and laughs out loud. "My hooker? Sorry for laughing Gina but that's a good one."

"Stop being an arsehole and just tell me."

"Okay. She's just a friend Gina." He is still smiling, and it is taking all my willpower not to smack him one.

"Right a friend. You looked like more than friends to me."

"Seriously Gina, stop with the jealousy. Anyone would think you were in love with me or something."

He laughs as he says this, but I am a little shocked at how embarrassed I am. I feel my face grow hot and I can't look at him. Oh my God am I in love with him? His expression changes when he looks at me.

"Oh no Gina please, I was joking. I'm sorry. Cerys is a good friend and my PA. She's also married... to a woman."

Oh God I feel like such an idiot. Sitting down on the chair in the hallway, I drop my head in my hands. "What the hell is wrong with me?"

I feel him kneel down on the floor beside me. "Gina look at me." His deep blue eyes search my face. "There is nothing wrong with you. You deserve much better than this Gina. I promised you I would make you happy and all I have done is make you miserable."

He takes my hand. "Come, I want to tell you what happened to me." He stands and pulls me to my feet.

"Why now and not this afternoon?"

"I used your appointment and went to see Nate. He convinced me to talk to you. He said it was only fair that I told you because you're involved in this mess now. I owe you that much Gina. All you've ever been is open with me. I guess it's my turn now. Come and sit in the living room and I'll get us a drink, we're going to need it."

I follow him into the living room and take a seat

on one of the big sofas.

"Just water for me, I've had enough of the hard stuff."

Steven returns carrying a glass of whisky that looks like it has about five measures in it. He sits down next to me. Handing me my glass he holds his up in a toast.

"Cheers babe."

I take a sip of the cold liquid. It feels amazing sliding down my throat.

"Cheers."

"I'm bloody scared to tell you all this Gina. Scared in case you hate me afterwards."

"Steven please, I won't hate you. I could never hate you."

He takes a deep breath and a large gulp of whisky and his body tenses. His jaw is set, and I can see a little nerve moving in his cheek. His voice is shaky when he begins.

"After my mum died, I was put in foster care. Obviously, I was a baby, so I don't remember that, but I've seen my social work file, so I know what happened. My so-called dad didn't want to know me when I was born and wouldn't let my mum name him on my birth certificate because he was already married. But my mum made a will and named him as my father in that."

He twists his glass nervously in his hands and I can see the tortured look in his eyes. My head is starting to clear, and I think a headache is imminent.

"So they ended up sending me to live with him and his wife, but they split up soon after that. She was obviously pissed about his affair and didn't want to bring up someone else's kid. We moved out and went to live with his mum, she was an old hag. I think she hated me. When I was seven, he took me to London to live because he had work down there as a scaffolder. That's when the shit really hit the fan and my life got fucked beyond belief."

He drinks what is left of his whisky, turning the empty glass in his hands.

"Are you really sure you want to hear all this Gina?"

I nod, and he continues.

"Things were okay for a little while when we first moved there. He had stopped drinking as much and was actually taking care of me like a dad should, well as good as I could have hoped for. That all changed after about three months. He started drinking again and was bringing prostitutes home. Every time I asked who they were he told me they were my new mum and would always laugh at me. They were never mothers in their lives. Most of them were dirty junkies. I only ever saw most of them once. Except one who came back a few times. She was nice. Not dirty and smelly like the others. The night she died was the worst time of my life and I still replay the scene over and over in my head. I see it in my dreams and to this day I still feel like I could have done something to stop it. I know an eight-year-old child has no control over a grown man, but it doesn't stop me feeling guilty."

Steven picks at some imaginary fluff on the couch but doesn't look at me. I stay silent.

"He had gone out and left me in the flat with her. He went to get more booze. It was the first time he had left me with anyone. Usually he would just leave me on my own when he went out. I actually became good at looking after myself. She helped me get ready for bed and gave me some dinner and we watched some TV together. I remember thinking at the time that she would be a good mum. We'd fallen asleep on the couch by the time he dragged his drunk arse home and he was in a foul mood. He went mental when he saw us asleep. I can still remember hearing her screaming. That sound has haunted me ever since. He dragged her off the couch by her hair."

His eyes are filled with tears when he looks at me.

"She had beautiful long brown hair and he was pulling it so hard and she was screaming so loud. I tried to stop him, but he punched me in the face and when I fell to the floor, he kicked me in the ribs. He shouted that I was nothing but a little scrounging bastard and that I had ruined his life. He said he hated me and wished I was dead. When she said she was going to social services about him that sent his rage sky high. He got hold of the back of her head and..."

He shakes his head as tears run down his cheeks. I want to reach out and hug him and tell him everything will be okay.

"He fucking murdered her right there in front of me Gina. He smashed her skull off the coffee table. There was blood everywhere, then it all went quiet and he walked out. He left me alone with her dead body. I was only a wee boy I didn't know what to do. I should have called the police, but I was too scared and I didn't want to lose her. She had taken care of me."

His body is shaking and I reach out and hold his hand. I feel physically sick.

"I cleaned the blood off her face and brushed her hair so that she would look nice again. He never came back and it was two days later when the police found us. I didn't want to leave her, but they made me. They didn't even know I existed. He never told them he had a son when they arrested him."

His voice cracks.

"She was the closest thing I had to a mum.

Someone who liked me, wanted to help me."

His head drops and he is consumed by grief. The sobs come in great waves. All I can do is hold him. I pull him close to me and wrap my arms around him. I am so shocked and think about how angelic he must have looked, how innocent. How could any parent do that to a child? Why is he not still in jail? We stay wrapped up like that for a long time. When his breathing relaxes and evens out, I know he has fallen asleep.

"I am so sorry." I whisper. "I promise I'll take care of you."

CHAPTER 18

WOW! THIS MUST BE what it feels like to fly. My body is weightless and I am floating. Floating on a cloud. THUD.

"Shit!"

My eyes fly open. It takes me a second to realise I am not flying but being carried.

"Sorry baby, I didn't mean to wake you." Steven's voice is soft. "I was putting you to bed. Do you want to stay over?"

"Mmm hmm."

It's all I can muster. I am so tired and my head is thumping. I snuggle into his strong arms and let him carry me. We reach the bedroom and he sets me down on the bed. Kneeling down on the floor in front of me he looks up at me.

"Thank you Gina."

"For what?"

"For listening and not judging."

"Steven, why on earth would you think I would judge you? You were only a child. Parents are supposed to protect you, love you unconditionally."

I put my hand on his cheek and caress his beautiful face. "Thank you for telling me. I know that took a lot."

"You needed to know Gina. He is dangerous and is obviously still holding a grudge. I was the only witness to that murder and I was the one who made sure he was jailed. He shouldn't be out of jail and he certainly shouldn't be anywhere near me."

He shakes his head.

"I can't believe after all this time he is still trying to ruin my life again. I swear I will fucking kill him if he lays a finger on you. I would go to the ends of the earth to keep you safe Gina."

He pulls me close and kisses the top of my head. I am taken aback by how loving and caring his gestures are. I know that man is dangerous, but I trust Steven when he says that he will protect me.

"Are you staying the night?"

"Of course I will."

"Get some sleep then Gina. I have some work I

need to do, and I don't sleep much anyway."

He pulls out the blue Uni t-shirt again and lays it down on the bed.

"Stand up."

I oblige, and he proceeds to strip me down to just my knickers and pulls the T-shirt over my head. He disappears for a moment and I think to myself that I should maybe get some painkillers. The hangover is kicking in and my head is thumping. As if telepathic Steven emerges from the bathroom with a glass of water and two shiny white pills.

"For your head," he says handing them to me. All I can do is smile at him. Looking into his eyes I can see the torment in them. But I also see compassion and love. He has been through hell, my dad was right, he has done well for himself despite all that. I feel guilty for having the upbringing I did.

"Gina. Earth to Gina. You okay?"

"Yes, sorry, just thinking. Now gimme those painkillers my head is about to explode. What time is it?"

"It's eleven thirty or there about."

"Wow, we must have slept for a long time."

"Gina, I think I had four hours of unbroken sleep. That's probably more than I've had at one time in my whole adult life.

He bows his head and whispers: "Thank you."

Leaning forward I kiss the top of his head. I think being able to tell me as much as he did has helped him in more ways than he realises. He will probably never fully appreciate how much he has helped me. He has saved me from myself and I will always be grateful for that.

"Right missy," he laughs at me as I scowl at his now infamous words. "Sleep. You've had a heavy day and that alcohol needs to work its way out of your system."

"Yes sir," I say with a mock salute. The look that flashes across his face is mischievous and slightly dark.

"Hmmmm." He murmurs. "I think I like hearing that on your lips Gina, say it again."

This time I try my best sultry tone. "Yes sir." It comes out very Marilyn Monroe and he shakes his head.

"Fuck me Gina, I am getting out of here before you turn me into a nervous wreck."

I smile as I lie down on the massive comfy bed. He leans over me and kisses me ever so softly. His lips linger a moment.

"Sleep gorgeous."

I watch him walk out of the room and the overwhelming need to sleep takes hold of me. My eyes feel heavy and I sigh out a long exhausted breath. I have had a lot to process today and my head hurts from too many gins. I feel myself drift off, the last thought in my head is that I am safe and happy again.

***

I have been awake for about ten minutes. Lying here in the dark in this cosy bed I am so warm that I really don't want to move but I need to pee. I get out and make a run for the loo. On the way back I kick the leg of the chair by mistake and fall onto my knees shouting:

"Ahhh…Fuck, Fuck, Fuck!"

My big toe is throbbing, white hot pain. I hobble over to the bed and am about to pull the covers back up over me when the bedroom door flies open.

"Gina are you okay? What happened?"

The light behind Steven illuminates him like some sort of God.

"Kicked the chair. Think I've broken my toe." I am wincing in pain and he is smiling at me.

"Jesus Gina, I thought the ceiling was coming in. Let me see."

Tentatively I pull the covers back. He holds my toe and moves it about a bit. It is sore, but I know myself it is not broken.

"You're fine, I'll get some ice."

He comes back with a bag from the freezer and places it on my foot when I see what it is, I laugh so hard I think I might pass out. I don't even notice the cold.

"What are you laughing at? It was all I could find."

"Mini sausage rolls. Are we having a wee buffet in bed?" I don't know why I find it so funny.

"Shut it you, they are my guilty pleasure. Please don't tell anyone it could ruin my reputation as a suave and sophisticated man about town." His boyish grin is infectious and I am starting to forget my pain. I reach over to grab my phone. I realise that it is still dark outside, but I feel like I have slept for an age.

"It's nearly six o'clock," says Steven.

"I assume you are wide awake now so would you like a coffee?"

"Yes please. I'll get you downstairs. I'm going to have a quick shower first if you don't mind."

"Not at all." He removes the bag and lifts my toe to his mouth. Gently placing a kiss on it he looks at me with a dark, passionate stare. His warm breath against my cold skin. Now, I'm not into all that foot fetish stuff but my God this is so bloody hot. Sensations are coursing through my body like live wires jumping and sparking. Putting my foot back on the bed he gets up and walks out the door, the last glimpse I get is his peachy ass in well-fitted jeans.

A shiver runs through me. He intrigues me. I am falling for him and it doesn't sit all that easily with me. The feeling that all this could come crashing down around me at any moment frightens me. I glance down at my phone pressing the home button and realise that it has run out of battery.

"Bugger it." I mutter to myself. I hate not having access to my phone. It's like I'm missing a limb. Pathetic really but my phone was my best friend for months. I shower and pull on a robe I found hanging on the back of the bathroom door. It's miles too big but is the snuggliest thing I have ever worn. Wrapping a towel round my hair I make my way down to the kitchen. Walking through the living room I stop short as I look into the kitchen. Steven is standing with his back to the door wearing a pair of light over washed jeans and a white shirt. His feet are bare. The clothes are a perfect fit on him and show off his sculpted body to perfection. It takes all my will power not to jump him, he looks so sexy.

"Taking in the scenery Gina?"

His question makes me jump, especially since he says it without even turning around. I feel my face redden as he turns to look at me.

"Coffee is ready. Are you hungry gorgeous?"

I am starting to love the way he calls me that, the

188

way it falls so easily from his mouth and wraps me up.

"No coffee is fine… handsome."

Trying out my own term of endearment all I can do is laugh at myself. His goofy smile says it all. Yes, it sounded ridiculous coming out of my mouth. As I walk towards him, he grabs me and kisses me so lightly it is like butterfly wings batting against my lips. I am swept off my feet every time he touches me so when he takes his lips away my eyes stay closed as I savour his touch. The tingling sensation travelling all over my body. No one else has ever made me feel this way before.

"Mmmmm babe I'm sorry but I have to go in to the office this morning." He sounds genuinely disappointed at this prospect and that is mirrored in my expression.

"But only this morning." He gives me that wink. "I'm going to see your dad this afternoon, I was hoping you would come too."

Well duh!

"Of course I'll come I need to go and pick up some stuff from their house and go home today anyway. I haven't been back in my house since Saturday."

I also need to see mum and arrange for her to come flat hunting with me. I want to get my life in order and getting out of that house is my next step. The first being this beautiful soul standing before me. His smile is endearing and infectious. I smile back at him as he hands me my coffee.

"Deal. We'll grab some lunch then head over. Are you good to wait here for me? I'll be finished for around noon."

I nod as I take a sip of my coffee, hatching a little plan as I do.

"Okay, I'm off to get ready."

He puts his hand behind my head, in my hair, and leans in to me so that his mouth brushes my ear: "Until lunch special girl. I am getting out of here because I know you are naked under that robe and I really need to get some work done."

And off he goes as a smile lights up my face.

CHAPTER 19

'HOW LONG WILL YOU be? Gx'

'I'll be there for noon. You missing me babe? x'

Laughing to myself I quickly type a response.

'Don't flatter yourself. I have lunch sorted so I'll see you when you get here. x'

Within seconds I have a reply and I can't help but smile as his words send a tingle through me.

'Please tell me it's you naked on a silver platter. If it is I'll be there in a minute. x'

'Yeah funny-man. See you at 12. Gx'

Putting an end to the conversation before it turns smutty, I set about fixing lunch. I have spent the morning getting my bearings in this vast apartment. It is absolutely stunning with high ceilings and massive windows. Every room is tastefully decorated and I have found the one I like best. It is an informal lounge area just off the main entrance that has two big sofas and a snooker table. There is also a rather expensive sound system next to a massive TV. The floor is a cream tile and the walls are a dark grey colour. It just feels...right.

I find what I am looking for in the freezer. Now to work out the oven. The thing is massive and there are three doors. Surely it can't be that hard, although, compared to my crappy effort of a cooker at home this looks like a spaceship. I run my hand down the shiny black surface next to the doors and as I do a whole myriad of lights, numbers and icons burst to life. 'GOOD MORNING STEVEN' scrolls along the top in bright blue letters. This thing is amazing. It's like the Star ship Enterprise.

"Beam me up Scotty."

My belly is rumbling as I line the little morsels up on a baking tray which looks brand new. In fact every pot, pan, tray and utensil in this kitchen looks brand new. Doesn't he cook? I decide I need some music. I noticed earlier that each room has an iPod dock, so I pull out my iPhone and attach it to the dock in the kitchen. Flicking to the playlists I decide to do a random shuffle and hope for the best.

The strains of an electric guitar pour from speakers and I laugh loudly as Marvin Gaye starts singing 'let's get it on'. Realising Steven will be back soon I start to gather up my stuff to take over to mum and dads. As I head out of the kitchen, I can still hear Marvin crooning away. The whole place is wired for sound, this is amazing. As I grab the last of my things from the bedroom the song changes and I now have banjos and a guitar as Mumford and Sons pipes up. Heading towards the stairs and singing: "I will wait, I will wait for you," at the top of my voice until I am stopped by the sound of a male voice singing along accompanied by the piano. I peek over the banister and see Steven playing the piano and singing. Filled with delight I take the last steps two at a time and sing along with Steven. He plays like a professional and his voice... wow. Moving over on the seat he beckons me to sit beside him all the while his fingers work overtime on the keys moving fast and fluidly and as the song finishes, he turns to me with a huge smile on his face.

"Hey gorgeous," he says as he pulls me to him and plants a delicious kiss on my lips. It's like Guy Fawkes every time he kisses me.

"Hey yourself songbird," I say a little breathless.

"I was going to ask you if you played when you

got back but I guess you already answered that. That was amazing."

"I learned to play when I was at Uni. I've always had a love of piano music. It got me through some shitty times when I was younger and I wanted to see how it felt to run my fingers over the keys."

That explains the piano but what about the voice.

"Your singing voice is beautiful too."

"One of my many talents babe." He winks cheekily at me.

"Now Missy," he laughs.

"If I am not mistaken, that is the smell of the best lunch anyone has ever made me."

"You're early, you weren't supposed to be here till noon, and it's only ten to."

I am a little put out by his early arrival, I wanted lunch to be a surprise.

"Well I was finished early and I was intrigued when you said you were doing lunch. Now woman, feed me." He smirks at me and when I go to stand up, he swats me hard on my bum. The look on his face is so sexy it is seriously turning me on. I turn away, my face flushed, and yes, I am smiling. It is a nice feeling.

Pulling the tray out of the oven and placing the food on to plates I glance at the mini sausage rolls. Oh God I feel stupid now. This is not lunch; it looks more like food you would serve at a kid's birthday party or a bloody funeral. With that thought my happy mood dissipates. As I set the tray down, I feel the old familiar tug of tears, sorrow and guilt. NO! I won't let it happen. I want to be happy; I need to be happy again.

"Come on to fuck Gina!" I hear myself screaming at the top of my voice. I am so annoyed with myself. I thought I was getting somewhere and then just one stupid little thing triggers the guilty feelings in the pit of my stomach. It is always there, under the surface, just waiting to emerge. I don't think I will ever be free.

"Gina, are you okay?" I turn and see Steven standing in the doorway, a look of concern and confusion etched on his face.

"No I'm fucking not. What are you doing with me? What is this anyway?" I gesture with my hand between us. "I mean come on, look at you. Why would you want to compete every day with the ghost of my husband?"

I shake my head and put my hands up in the air as if motioning towards the heavens. "Thanks a lot Aiden."

As inappropriate as it is, I feel the beginnings of a little laugh coming up from my belly. Before long I am in full-blown hysterics. I look back at Steven and he is smiling but his expression is still confused.

"Why are you laughing?"

He asks as he cocks his head to one side. The music has changed through a few songs now and the dulcet tones of Kenny Rogers are filling the air.

"Why did he have to die? Why couldn't he have just left me? Then I could hate him and not feel guilty every time anything goes good for me."

I bow my head. "This isn't fair on you Steven. I guess I'm just not meant to be happy."

In a second, he is in front of me and has my hand in his. "Gina, do you really believe that? That you're not meant to be happy? You were happy once weren't you? You said so yourself. When Aiden was here did he make you happy?"

I have to think about that for a second. Was I really happy? Maybe I was to start with. I really loved Aiden but the more and more I think about it I wonder whether we were just going through the motions. The little things that have come to light since he died have me questioning our life together.

"I don't know Steven, I just don't know."

The fact that I am falling in love with Steven hits me like a ton of bricks. I have fallen hard and fast. I want to put on my shoes and run away from all of this. I've only known him for just over a week. How the hell can I feel this way already?

"You know what I think Gina?" He asks with a little smile playing at his lips. "I think you're scared. You're scared of how you feel about me, about us. It's guilt. It wasn't your fault that Aiden died Gina. You can keep punishing yourself for the rest of your life, but it won't change a thing. I learned that a long time ago. I blamed myself for everything that happened to me. My mum dying, my dad fucking hating me, ending up in care. It took a long time to come to terms with the fact that I wasn't to blame for all that."

"But it *was* my fault." My voice falters. I have never told anyone what happened the night Aiden died. The whole reason he was out on that bloody bike that night was because of me.

"No Gina it..."

I hold up my hand. "Yes it was. You don't know what happened. I've never told anyone. Not even Nate."

I can feel my tears welling up and with a blink of my eyes they cascade down my cheeks.

In a swift and gentle move Steven catches my tears with his thumb. "Hey baby, don't cry. I think it would help if you spoke to Nate about this. You need to clear your head; this guilt's not good for you. You know there is nothing you could have done to stop this happening, don't you?"

197

"I accused him of having an affair." My words are barely a whisper.

"Do you want to talk about it?" His eyes are full of sincerity

"Aiden had been acting strange for a while and the night he died he came home really late and picked a fight for no reason. He was spouting some crap about our money troubles and told me he thought he was going to get laid off, as if it was my entire fault. My photography business was failing and I wasn't bringing in enough money. He said he basically felt like he was carrying me. I had a great little studio a few years ago and was doing really well, but like everything right now most people want to do these things cheaper. My assistant was the first to go then I had to give up the studio. My heart just wasn't in it after that.

Aiden called me a failure and said I was spoiled. He said that I never had to work for anything because mummy and daddy would always be there to bail me out. I was furious with him for that. My mum and dad helped get me started in my business, but I paid them back as soon as I had made enough money. I asked him if he still loved me and he just shrugged his shoulders and said he couldn't listen to my whining anymore. I asked him if there was someone else, did he love someone else. He threw a fit and called me an ungrateful bitch and said, 'how dare I ask him that'. I told him to fuck off and get out of my sight; I just couldn't believe he would speak to me like that. He never answered me just put on his bike gear and went off."

I put my head in my hands: "The last thing I said, or rather shouted at him as he stormed out the door, was that he was being a prick. We said some truly horrible things to each other and we can never take them back."

"Gina you need to tell Nate this. You're punishing yourself for no reason. If Aiden was here right now, I would punch him in the face."

My head shoots up.

"Excuse me, but who do you think you are to say that?"

"I'm someone who cares about you very much."

"But you didn't know Aiden, he wasn't normally like that, he loved me."

"Really? Then why couldn't he answer you? Why couldn't he just say he wasn't having an affair instead of turning it round on you? No Gina I'm sorry but it sounds like you were on to him and if you ask me, he got off lightly."

"How fucking dare you!" I scream and lift my hand to slap him, but he is too quick and grabs my wrist.

"Oh no you don't," he says with a smile and tugs my arm so that I fall into him. With his other hand he yanks my hair back so that my face is tilted towards his. It is just on the cusp of painful. His eyes are an intensely deep blue and I am so close to him I can see myself reflected in them. My breath is caught in my throat and before I can react, he claims my mouth. His kiss is rough and hot, and I am swept up in it. God this feels so good, so right.

His tongue pushes my lips apart and he deepens the kiss. I feel myself relax in his arms, my body responding to his as if it is the most natural thing in the world. Steven picks me up all the while never breaking contact and carries me into the living room. He moves towards the fireplace and sinks down onto a large faux fur rug. I feel safe with him. I feel like I belong here, like maybe I've always belonged here.

"Gina." Steven whispers my name and kisses me everywhere he removes a piece of my clothing. His hands are warm and as he trails them over my naked body, I feel goose bumps rise on my skin and my nipples tighten in response. His eyes catch mine and once again I am lost in those stunning blue pools.

"Gina you are so beautiful."

He sits back on his knees, never breaking eye contact with me, and undoes the first few buttons of his shirt. Leaving the rest he pulls the shirt over his head. His lightly tanned torso is gorgeously toned, and it takes my breath away. He is perfection, and he is here with me. He wants me. I can't fathom out why, what it is about me? Right now I don't care, I know what my body wants. He's like a drug and I am scared to admit to myself that I may be just a little bit addicted.

Steven raises an eyebrow and a sexy smile appears on his lips. Leaning over me he unbuttons his jeans. The rough denim against the soft skin of my inner thigh has me turning to mush right there on the rug. I am caught in this spell he has woven around me. His hot mouth takes one of my nipples and he sucks hard on it. I moan at the intense shocks making their way round my nervous system. I feel myself getting wetter and my body bucks when he gives a little nip with his teeth. Closing my eyes I try to savour it but before I can come down his hand is between my legs. In one fluid motion his finger is inside me hitting my sweet spot straight away. The sensation is like a wave carrying me away and I can't fight it, I have to go with it. My body is screaming at me as if it is on the edge of a giant waterfall about to go over.

"Look at me Gina," Steven says, and I open my eyes. He presses the heel of his hand down and my clit sparks and pulses.

"Let go Gina," he says as he adds another finger and presses again, and my wanton body responds. I can feel every single pulse and throb of my muscles against his fingers.

"Oh God Gina, I can't wait any longer, I need to be inside you. I want to feel your cunt doing that to my cock."

His words make my muscles clench. He pushes his jeans just low enough to free himself and he takes me by surprise as he thrusts himself deep inside. I grasp his shoulders and hold on for dear life as he thrusts in and out. I meet his thrusts with my own and before long I am wound up to tipping point.

"Oh God Steven I'm coming, please, harder."

He thrusts into the depths of me and the orgasm that takes hold this time is so intense I feel light headed. I feel him slow slightly, then speed up again as he finds his release shouting my name. As the air returns to normal we lie side by side on the rug. Steven reaches up and pulls a fur lined throw from the sofa over us. I am sated, my eyelids heavy.

"I think I'm in love with you Gina."

Steven's words hang in the air and all I can do is smile at him. I know I feel the same but it's going to take time for me to be able to say it back.

CHAPTER 20

THE ONLY THING I can say about the last few hours is that my mum can certainly put on a spread. Good God you would have thought the bloody queen was coming for dinner. I was ever so glad that we didn't eat those sausage rolls before we left Steven's apartment otherwise we may have had to be rolled out the door. Steven and dad had their meeting in dad's office and mum pounced on me the moment I set foot in the kitchen alone. She was all *'I'm so glad you're moving on, what's he like? How are you getting along?'* I told her it was early days and yes, I liked him a lot, but we would have to see where it went.

After dinner, we said our goodbyes. Mum and I decide to meet up on Friday, so she can help me look for a new place. Steven has, of course, offered to give me a lift home. I am a little embarrassed that he will see the pokey little house I live in given the huge apartment he has. My mum and dad are thrilled about Steven. I know they like him, but I think the fact that I am moving on with my life is what is making them so happy. I look at Steven and take in his perfectly sculpted jaw line. He has a beautiful profile, manly yet elegant. He smiles at me; he knows I am looking at him.

"Gina are you determined to burn a hole in the side of my face?" His smile widens and I can see the tiny flex of the muscle by his cheek.

"Just admiring you from afar," I say with a smile.

"You're not that far away," he says as he glances at me and rests his hand on my knee. Oh this is nice, strange but nice.

"No, I'm not." I put my hand over his and keep it there the whole way home, even when he has to change gears. As we approach my little house, I notice that the estate agent has been and there is a for sale board in the front garden. I get a little pang in my chest, but I know this is for the best. Steven stops at the kerb because there is only room in the driveway for my little VW Golf. It really pales in comparison to this beast of a car. Oh my neighbour's curtains will be twitching.

"Would you like to come in for a coffee?"

"I can't babe I have a meeting to go to, but I would like to take you out tomorrow. You up for that?"

"Of course. Where are we going?"

"Not telling you, it's a surprise." He gives me a smile and a wink.

"Oh I love surprises."

I say unconvincingly. I bloody hate surprises. I've never been good at Christmas and birthdays. I always went on a treasure hunt to try and find my presents. When I think about Steven and his horrible life I wonder if he ever had a proper Christmas.

"Right it's a date. I'll pick you up here at 7.00."

He leans in and kisses me. His lips lingering he whispers: "I don't want to go."

"I don't want you to go either."

"I really need to get to this meeting, it's too important to ditch. I'll call you later babe okay?"

"Till then handsome." I turn to him as I get out of the car and try to wink. All I manage is a blink and we both laugh.

"Okay 7.00 on the dot tomorrow. See you then babe."

As I close the door, I give a little wave and he blows me a kiss then he is off.

Entering the hallway of the house the cold hits me

full force, I haven't been back since Saturday. I flick the thermostat on high and head for the kitchen to make a coffee. The answer machine light is blinking with a little F signalling that there is no room for any new messages. Goodness I have been popular. The first message is from Charlie.

"Hey babe, just letting you know I'm home. I'm texting you too just in case you ended up away home with lover boy. Ha, speak soon."

The next two are hang-ups. As I go through the marketing calls and more hang ups, I get the feeling that something is wrong. Six hang ups are not normal. As I listen to the seventh message a chill runs up my spine when as a sinister laugh escapes from the machine. It sounds evil and I can't tell if it is male or female. Instinctively I delete the message. I don't ever want to hear that again. The next one is from Aiden's mum, Sandra, and my God is she not happy. The message was left yesterday.

"Gina, I don't know what you are playing at here, but you better call me as soon as you drag your slutty arse back home."

Oh my God! What the hell is she talking about? Does she know about Steven? But how? Has she seen the for-sale sign outside the house? She has never spoken to me like that before. I love Sandra to bits and I know Aiden's death affected her badly, no-one should outlive their kids, but it doesn't give her the right to speak to me like that. I decide to call her back later. Right now I need some space to think.

I head up to my bedroom and flick on the light. It takes me a moment to process the scene in front of me. Five sets of underwear are spread out on my bed. The drawer has been dumped on the floor along with the remaining contents. I look around the room in shock only to be confronted with writing scrawled in scarlet lipstick on the mirrored doors of my wardrobes. B I T C H; one letter on each of the five doors. Oh God. I feel the bile rise in my throat. Someone has been in my house. My first instinct is to call Steven.

"Hey babe I was just thinking about you. Couldn't get enough of me eh?" He laughs as a sob escapes from my mouth. "Gina what the fuck? Are you okay?"

"Oh Steven…I'm sorry." I can't say anything else.

"I'm coming to get you stay where you are. I'll be there in ten minutes. Can you tell me what's wrong?"

The fear is choking me and I can't speak.

"Right I won't be long. I'll stay on the line okay?"

The thoughts going through my mind are driving me crazy. Could Sandra have done this? Why would she? I know her message was nasty, but I could never imagine her doing something as disgusting as this, especially not to me. I hear Steven's voice at the bottom of the stairs.

"Gina, Gina, where are you? Help me out here."

I get up off the floor and run out the bedroom door. He is at the top of the stairs and I launch myself in to his arms.

"It's okay baby I'm here. Tell me what happened."

"Take a look." I open the bedroom door.

"What the fuck is this? Gina have you been robbed?"

In my haste to call Steven and my fear over the writing on the mirrors I didn't actually check if anything was missing.

"I don't know I haven't checked."

As he turns to look at me, he catches a glimpse of the mirrors and the colour drains from his face.

"Right, you're coming to stay with me Gina. I can't leave you here. Grab some stuff for a couple of days but try not to disturb anything if you can help it. I'm just going to make a few calls. Will you be okay?"

"Yes." I don't argue with him. I'm happy to leave. I really don't think I could stay here now. My personal space has been invaded and knowing someone was here freaks me out. I can hear Steven's muffled voice through the door and I move closer to try and make out what he is saying.

"...really sorry Debbie. I know but something came up. Can we reschedule? Tomorrow morning is good for me. Thanks Debbie, see you then."

He hangs up and moves on to another call

"Nick, Steven Parker. There's been a development. I'll email the details over shortly. I know Nick, but this is important. I need to know his whereabouts. Someone must know something. Right as soon as you speak to them let me know. Bye."

As he hangs up, I scurry away from the door and look busy. Oh God he thinks his dad is responsible for this. Surely he doesn't know where I live?

"You ready babe."

"Almost, I just need some undies. Oh erm..." I look at the strewn garments and turn to him.

"We'll go shopping. The shops are open late since it's nearly Christmas. Right let's go then."

"Hold on, shouldn't we call the police? I can't feel safe until I know what happened."

"It's all in hand. I've already made some calls. Are you ready?" I wonder why he doesn't mention the phone call.

"Yes I'm ready." I plaster a smile on my face, but my mind is in turmoil.

"Right let's get you out of here."

As the car starts up, I glance at the house one last

time. I think if I never came back here it wouldn't really bother me now. I have had enough. That message from Sandra was the last straw. I can't believe she would call me a slut, all I am doing is trying to get on with my life.

"I think I know who did this," I say as the car pulls away from the kerb. He keeps his eyes on the road.

"Who?"

"Aiden's mum."

"What?" His head snaps round to look at me.

"When I got home tonight, I had loads of messages and the one from Sandra was particularly nasty. She called me a slut and asked what the fuck I was playing at. I don't know if it is because she knows I am selling the house or if it's because she knows about you."

I am hoping now he will share his suspicions with me, but he doesn't.

"Are you sure it could be her? Why would she do something like that? Didn't she like you or something?"

"She did, she loved me. I don't know what her problem is? I'll need to speak to her, find out what's going on."

"I would wait a few days, let the police handle it. They'll probably need to come and speak to you; did you keep the answer phone message?"

"Yes. I didn't delete that one."

"What do you mean that one? Were there more?" His eyes are still on the road and when I turn to look at him, I see a little muscle in his cheek flexing.

"Just a load of marketing calls and some hang ups. There was one that was a bit strange, but it was probably just a wrong number."

"What did they say?"

"Nothing, it was just someone laughing, it may have been a man, but I couldn't tell. It was quite eerie but like I said it was probably a wrong number."

"Right, okay, I suppose it probably was."

I can't bear this withholding of information from me, so I ask him outright. "Steven do you think your dad has something to do with this?"

He sighs. "I really hope not Gina, but I already have people looking in to it, so we will know soon enough."

"Thank you. Not just for having people looking in to it but for telling me. It means a lot."

He puts his hand on mine and gives me a small smile. It's enough. I feel better knowing that he is working to keep me safe and because I know what he is thinking it makes that task a little easier.

CHAPTER 21

I WAKE TO DARKNESS. It just takes a second for
me to realise that I am in Steven's bed. I can hear
someone breathing next to me. For the first time since
we started...whatever this is...he is sleeping in the
same bed as me. I never found it strange before but
now that I think about it, it really is. I need to pee. I
get out of the bed as quietly as I can. I have on the
good old Glasgow Uni T-shirt that I have made my
own. I can't see a thing so I grab my phone from the
bedside table and press the home button so that my
screen lights up a pathway to the door. I use the toilet
downstairs because I don't want to wake Steven.
Splashing some water on my face I decide that I need
to call Charlie today. I have got to stay in touch with

her more and I need to tell her what has happened. Taking my phone I head to the kitchen. I am a little annoyed that it is just after four in the morning. I put on the muted lighting under the cupboards so I can see where I am going and what I am doing.

I have an email from an address I don't recognise. It has been sent to my business address which is strange since I haven't used it for months. Flicking on the all singing all dancing coffee machine I sit down on one of the bar stools and unlock the phone. It isn't a message at all but a grainy picture which has been crudely photo shopped. It is a picture of me and Steven outside my house from last night. Above our heads are the letters BITCH and next to me the sender has drawn gallows with the noose around my neck like hangman. Oh my God who the hell is doing this to me? What on earth have I done to deserve this? Does someone want me dead? The thought sends chills up my spine.

"Morning gorgeous." I am startled by Steven's voice and almost drop my phone.

"God you scared me."

"Sorry babe. I woke up and you weren't there. Or rather I woke up because you weren't there so I came to find you. And what a mighty fine find you are."

Standing in the doorway in a loose pair of pyjama trousers he almost takes my mind off the picture.

213

"I need to show you something but before I do, I need you to answer something for me. I want the truth Steven, don't even try to bullshit me okay."

He holds up a hand: "Whoa okay what's happened?"

"Do you really think your father is responsible for what happened at my house? Steven answer me, do you think it was him?"

"I did last night but after we got back here, I made some more calls and found out that he had been at some parole meetings down in London. He hasn't been in Scotland since you saw him last week."

"Oh right. So my theory about Sandra could be right then. God this is just too sad to even contemplate. Sandra and I were close but since Aiden died, I've only seen her a handful of times. I didn't want to see anyone. She was dealing with her own grief, I couldn't have handled hers on top of mine. Oh Steven, what am I going to do about her? I really don't want to get her in trouble. She doesn't deserve that."

"For God sake Gina, do you think you deserve to be treated like this? You've done nothing wrong. All you're doing is getting on with your life. She can't hold anything over you if you don't want her to. She probably can't let you go because you are the last link she has to her son. It's sad yes but it's not fair on

214

anyone."

As he walks closer to me, I breathe in his scent. I feel a spark whenever I smell him.

"I know I'm going to have to talk to her, but it'll be hard. Look, I found this on my phone this morning."

He studies the picture. "This is not fucking on Gina. I'm going to find out who is doing this. The police will be here later on this morning to talk to you about what happened at the house, you need to show this to them."

"Have they been to my house? "

"Of course they have. I'll do everything in my power to keep you safe Gina, but do you really think Sandra could be capable of this? I mean I know grief can do strange things to people but surely this is beneath her."

I know he is talking sense. I really don't think Sandra would do anything as nasty as that to me.

"No you're right, she couldn't have done this. I really don't know who it could be. I have never done anything to make someone hate me so much."

Steven shakes his head and comes towards me pulling me close to him. Kissing the top of my head he takes a deep breath.

"I meant what I said yesterday Gina. I am falling in love with you and it scares me that someone is trying to hurt you. It's especially frustrating because I don't know who is doing this, so I feel powerless to stop them."

"Steven." I whisper and I push back slightly so that I can look at him. "I feel the same."

He kisses my lips, a light butterfly kiss and murmurs against my mouth. "I love you Gina."

"I love you too Steven."

I feel tears form in my eyes, but they are happy tears. I can't believe this is real. I had all but written myself off and now I have someone to love and who loves me. This time will be different. I know it will.

"Come on let's make some toast and coffee and go and watch some TV. I'm not tired and I can't sleep without you there anyway."

As he goes to the cupboard and pulls out two mugs I ask: "Why don't you sleep much? Do you have insomnia?"

He doesn't turn around, instead I see his shoulders slump a little. "Every time I shut my eyes to sleep, I replay what my dad did over and over. It fills my dreams like a virus. I've taken to just having the odd catnap every now and then, at work or at my desk here. Usually that happens when I'm so exhausted I either don't dream or I just don't remember them. I've slept more next to you than I have in years Gina."

He turns and looks at me, his expression solemn. "I need you Gina, I really do. I've never really let anyone get this close to me."

"Come here." I beckon him over to me. Putting my arms round his neck and pulling him closer to me I stretch up on my tiptoes and whisper in his ear.

"I need you too my knight in shining armour."

He puts his arms round my waist and lifts me off my feet, kissing me hard enough that my lips swell. As he loosens his grip on me and I slide down his body, I hear the coffee machine buzz.

"Go and turn on the TV and I'll bring the coffee through. I have a little surprise for you later."

He me gives me a little wink and I smile at him and try to wink back, blinking both eyes and looking like I have something in them. I'll master it someday. He laughs and as I turn around to walk away, he smacks me on my behind.

We watch The Hitchhiker's Guide to the Galaxy and I must have fallen asleep before the end because when I open my eyes it is light. I am wrapped up in a fleece blanket on the sofa in the TV room. I can smell coffee and it makes my senses perk up. Standing up and pulling the blanket around my shoulders I go in search of a caffeine fix. I am a little disheartened when I see the kitchen is empty. There is a note stuck to the fridge door with a silver magnet.

Hey babe had to go into work.
The police will be here to see you around 11am.
Call me when they have been.
S x

Looking at the clock on the wall I notice that it is already almost eleven, so I quickly get dressed in jeans and a T-shirt. I am heading downstairs pulling my hair into a ponytail when I hear the intercom buzz. Pressing the button I say a tentative, "Hello."

The voice that comes back is as clear as if the person on the other end is standing next to me. "Hi there, we are looking for Georgina Connor. This is DI Fraser and DI Marshall."

"Ok I'll buzz you in."

I'm nervous as I open the door and hear the heavy footsteps of the police officers as they ascend the stairs. When they reach the door, I am startled by just how tall they are and I feel tiny next to them. The younger of the two extends his hand to me. "Ms Connor? I am DI Fraser, and this is DI Marshall. It's nice to meet you."

I shake his hand and then that of DI Marshall.

"Come in," I say with an awkward and not very convincing smile. I take a seat across from them both in the living room.

"We have been to your house and taken prints. We have some questions to ask you and we need a full set of prints from you to enable us to eliminate them from the scene. Does anyone live with you or visit on a regular basis? We need to know so we can eliminate any of them from our enquiries."

I shake my head. "No, just me."

That sounds so sad and pathetic.

"Steven may have touched something while he was there but there has been no one else in my house since...well..."

I shrug my shoulders. I am absolutely fed up thinking about how utterly desolate my life has been.

"Right you'll need to drop in to the station to get your fingerprints taken and it would be helpful if you could do that as soon as possible. I'll tell you this though we have only lifted two sets of prints and one of them are Mr Parker's."

I frown.

"It's okay Mr Parker's prints have already been taken. He came in first thing this morning. He knows the drill since he already had to do this once before after the break in at his office?"

I gather my composure and nod making a mental note to ask Steven later. "Okay I'll go later today. Can I go to any station? Or does it have to be the local one?"

"Any one will do. I'll give you the crime reference number. We spoke to Sandra Connor, she's your mother in law, right?"

I nod.

"We asked her about the voicemail message she left you. She has said that it was a heat of the moment thing and after checking out her whereabouts we are happy that she is not a suspect in this investigation. She would like to speak to you to explain her actions with regards to the phone call. I get the feeling she cares for you a lot Georgina."

"Call me Gina, please. I only get the Sunday name from my parents."

He gives a little laugh and nods.

"Yes Sandra does care for me. I know she's still grieving and will probably never stop."

"Well, based on our interview with her and her daughter, she is out of the picture as far as we are concerned. Is there anyone else you can think of that would do something like this? Anyone you have fallen out with recently or had a run in with?"

I shake my head. "No, I can count on one hand the people I've spoken to or seen over the last six months so no, no-one."

DI Marshall says: "There is probably no easy way to say this, but I don't think we'll find out who did this in all honesty. The lack of any substantial evidence means we can only take the investigation so far before we hit a dead end unless anything else turns up."

"I understand, honestly I do, and thank you for taking the time to investigate. I wasn't really expecting much to come out of it. I'm selling the house anyway, as you will be aware, so I probably won't really be back there to stay anyway."

"Your boyfriend did the best thing in contacting us," says DI Marshall. My eyes go wide and my heart thumps in my chest. My boyfriend. Is that what he is? I don't even know.

"You know there are so many crimes that go undetected because people don't call us in, so many criminals whose crimes may never have escalated if they had been caught earlier."

I think of Steven's dad and wonder how different things would be for Steven if maybe he had been stopped earlier when he was only into beating prostitutes up.

"I need to show you something." I flick open the email and hand the phone to him. DI Marshall looks at me, then back at the phone, then hands it to DI Fraser. He stares at it for a moment then looks at me with a troubled look on his face.

"This is progress Gina, this changes the course of the investigation now. It's a vital piece of evidence.

We will get the address checked out and all the other techy stuff that goes with it and we will be in touch as soon as we know more. They are going to need access to your email account. Could you write it down for me?"

DI Marshall stands as DI Fraser takes my email login details from me and finishes writing. "So Gina, if you think of anything else or if anything else happens to you please be sure to contact us. You've every right to feel safe and that's what we are here for."

"Thanks for coming to see me and for your help. I'm sure I will be fine, but yes if anything else happens I will call."

"Right we'll get on then." DI Fraser says and hands me back my phone as both of them head for the door.

"Take care Gina."

"Thanks."

Closing the door after them I lean against it letting out the longest sigh. DI Fraser's words tumble around in my brain. 'Your boyfriend.' We haven't even been on a date yet, so I really don't think that's what he is. I am so lost in my thoughts that the high pitched shrill of my phone ringing makes me jump. Pulling it out of my pocket I see that it is Steven.

"Hey." I answer, smiling.

"Hey babe. Have the police been yet?"

"Yes they've just left. They didn't think they would find out who it was until I showed them the picture and then they were quite positive about it."

"Well they know what they're doing so let's leave them to it. Anyway you need to go and get yourself ready. The wardrobe in the bedroom has a little something in it for you. I'll see you tonight."

CHAPTER 22

THE WARDROBE IN STEVEN'S bedroom is huge.
It's not a wardrobe it's a whole room. There is a free-
standing clothes rail in the middle with five black suit
bags hanging from it and five shoe boxes underneath.
Stuck to the front of the first suit bag is a large cream
coloured envelope with my name written in beautiful
calligraphy. I carefully peel it off. The paper feels
thick and luxurious and there is a note inside.

Hi Gorgeous
There is an outfit in each clothes bag and shoes to
match underneath.
Choose an outfit to wear today. You are going
shopping.

*I want you to go to Frasers and head for the
personal shopper.*
Ask for Carolina. She will be expecting you.
*She will give you her services for as long as you
need them today.*
*She will also give you the list of other things I have
planned for you.*
Enjoy babe and spend as much as you want.
Sx

Oh wow! What do I say to that? Attacking the
first bag I open it up and find a jade green slash neck
top and a pair of black shorts. They feel luxurious and
I daren't look at the labels in case I faint. I remove all
the other outfits and stand back to have a look. There
is a lovely knitted jumper dress in a beautiful crimson
colour, a pair of over washed ripped jeans and a
Calvin Klein T-shirt, a pair of straight leg black
trousers and a white sheer blouse. The last one has an
internal opaque white bag and there is another note
stuck to that one. Inside are a few pieces of red velour
material with a white feather trim. When I take it out
of the clothes bag, I am a little shocked. It is a tiny
sexy Santa outfit complete with hat, long gloves, red
and white stripy stockings and a feather garter. Oh
God, I can't wear this to go shopping in. '*Oh for God
sake Gina, of course he doesn't want you to go*

shopping in this'. I read the little note.

This one is for my eyes-only babe.
Sx

Oh my, I feel my face flush as red as the dress. I have never, in my life, worn anything like this. Running my fingers over the velour and feathery softness I wonder what it would be like against my body. I decide to try it on for a laugh. Five minutes later I am standing in front of the full-length mirror staring at myself. My God I could have been sewn into this it fits like a glove. It hugs in all the right places and is very flattering on my curves. I have a fleeting thought but shake my head and dismiss it. I wonder to myself what shoes you would wear with this. I check the shoeboxes to see what there is. The first one is a pair of patent green sandals with a three-inch heel. Hmm these will be for the shorts and top ensemble. The second box has a pair of light grey Converse. Right for the jeans and T-shirt. The third box has a pair of bright red super shiny shoe boots. Oh my God they are gorgeous and so sexy. Looking inside I gasp at the name tag. They are Gucci. These are bloody expensive shoes. With the red shoes on my feet I feel very tall and when I look at myself in the mirror a little smile plays at my lips. Yes, I feel sexy.

Maybe I will go with my first instincts…why not?

Rummaging in my makeup bag I find a bright red lipstick and put it on along with the Santa hat. Wow! I look good. Before I chicken out, I grab my phone point it at the mirror and take a picture.

I immediately text it to Steven with the caption:

'Merry Xmas babe xx'

I am not one for taking selfies, but this picture is for one pair of eyes only. Oh no! I just hope and pray he has his phone in his pocket and no one else sees it. Oh God now I'm panicking. What if he's in a meeting and his phone is in front of him and someone sees it. Oh shit shit shit! This is why I don't usually do things like this. I am about to die from embarrassment and the ensuing panic attack when my phone buzzes.

"Hello."

"Jesus fucking Christ Gina. I just had to excuse myself from a room full of people." His tone is playful and sexy as hell and I offer up my thanks that he is not mad.

"Really, why would that be?"

He lets out a low rumbling laugh. "You're a naughty girl Gina. Do you know how hard it is to talk to the Japanese in the first place without having to try and stave off a hard-on?"

"Oh I'm sorry Steven I didn't realise you were in a meeting."

"Hey, did I say I didn't like it? I just wish I were there. You wouldn't have them on long believe me."

I am getting a little turned on. An idea pops into my head and I know it's not like me but hey I'm feeling lucky and rather naughty, so I give it whirl.

"Where are you right now?"

"In my office, why?"

"Are you alone?"

"Yes, again why?"

"Where is everyone else?"

"In the meeting room having coffee. Gina why are you being so cryptic?"

"Good stay where you are, I'm going to call you back."

Before he can say anything, I hang up. Selecting the FaceTime function on my phone I call him back. My hands are trembling, I have never been so brazen in my life until I met Steven, but this feels so naughty and I am getting hornier by the second. I place my phone on the little table in front of me. As the call connects all I can see is darkness and the little box with my image in it. Thinking I have done something wrong I step closer to my phone but before I can get to it a light flicks on in the background. Steven is on my screen. He is sitting on his chair at his desk with his phone propped up. He says nothing. I was feeling really brave until now. Here goes nothing….

Facing the screen I take off one of the gloves, peeling it slowly down my arm. When it is off completely, I hold it out between two fingers and drop it looking seductively at him. I do the same with the other. Next, I turn my back and slowly start to ease the dress down my body, turning my head to the screen as I push it down over my hips. Incidentally I have no underwear on. Once the dress is over my hips, I let it fall to the floor and step out of it. Now I am only wearing the striped stockings, garter, red boots and Santa hat.

"Turn around Mrs Clause." Steven's voice comes through the phone. I turn to the screen consciously holding my belly in. As I look at the screen, I see that Steven has changed his position and is sitting further back. I can't see below his desk, but I can sure as hell guess why his arm is moving the way it is. It is making me even hornier knowing he is masturbating watching me.

"Fuck Gina." His voice is a deep growl. "You are fucking ruining me. Make yourself come for me Gina."

I think back to the first time I did that in his kitchen and how much it had turned him on. This, I feel, is even naughtier; he can't touch me. I want to see him come apart for me, because of me.

"Hold on. Just a second," I say as I leave the

room, quickly pulling my iPad out of my bag and hooking it up to the dock in the bedroom. I choose a love song playlist and the sultry strains of Otis Redding come through the speakers. I dash back into the closet and take my stance in front of the phone again. As the music starts, I close my eyes and sway my hips. Running my hands over my body moving to the music. I can hear Steven's breathing getting heavier. I don't think I am going to last long here and as my fingers skim over my pubic bone I feel shivers run up my spine. Slipping a finger inside myself I feel my legs almost give way. God this is hot as hell. Moving my finger in and out I press the heel of my hand against my clit and I am soaring. Just knowing what Steven is doing behind that desk as he watches me is bringing me so quickly to orgasm that I really don't think I will last the length of this song.

Opening my eyes and looking at the phone I see Steven staring straight at me his hand vigorously pumping. He moves the phone so that I can see what he is doing to himself. Oh my God this is so naughty and hot. I add another finger and that is it. I am gone, the orgasm ripping through me is blinding. I sink to my knees with one hand on the floor to steady myself. I can still feel the muscles pulsing round my fingers. In the distance I hear Steven's voice. It is low and sounds almost pained, "Oh fuck, Gina, fuck, fuck!"

I look up and see he has his eyes shut, his head thrown back against the chair. When I have finally come down from my high, I stand up and grab a robe from one of the hooks. It smells of Steven. Picking up my phone and looking into the screen I see Steven has picked up his phone as well.

"My God woman, I so wish I didn't have to be at the office right now. I really want to come home and fuck you till dawn."

I smile back shyly. "I take it this is an important meeting you are having."

"Major and I can't get out of it. In fact tea break is over and I really need to get back to them. Go and do your shopping and I will see you later. And Gina, that was sexy as fuck by the way."

He has a huge grin plastered on his face and I am proud of the fact that I put it there.

"Yeah it was. Gotta love the smart phone eh?"

He laughs. "Right babe I need to go. See you later."

He blows me a kiss and I reciprocate and we both hang up. I turn to the clothes rail still grinning like a fool. I choose the jeans and t-shirt since shopping always involves a lot of walking and I want to get something really sexy for tonight. I'll be wearing heels then, so I want to save my feet.

CHAPTER 23

ON MY WAY INTO town I make a detour to the police station to get the fingerprints out of the way. It only took five minutes. I gave them the crime reference number and they took me into a little room where they scanned my prints into a machine and that was it. I don't really know what I was expecting. I feel better knowing that is out of the way and as I walk through the doors of Frasers, I have a smile on my face. I go to the personal shopper desk and ask for Carolina.

"I'm Carolina, you must be Gina. It's lovely to meet you."

She is very tall and slender and has perfectly sculpted eyebrows. Her makeup is flawless and her dark chestnut hair is swept up in a tight French roll. She looks like she just stepped out of a fashion magazine.

"Come this way and we'll get started."

She leads me towards a doorway at the back of the store. Inside is a huge changing room filled with a flowery perfume. Carolina beckons me to sit on a plush plum velvet covered chaise and hands me a glass of pink champagne. This is the kind of shopping I like. In addition to the chaise there is a massive couch and two double sized cubicles with plum velvet curtains

"I've been asked to give you this," Carolina says as she hands me a thick cream envelope.

"I'll give you five minutes and then we can get started okay?"

"Okay thanks."

When she has gone, I open the envelope. Inside is a piece of cream paper with the same writing as the notes back at the apartment. I read it slowly.

Hey Gorgeous
Hope you enjoy your day.
Read these points one at a time and do as you are told.

1. Friends are like bras, close to the heart and

always there for support.
Open the curtain on the dressing room.

Oh goody sounds like I can get started with the underwear then. I stand up and pull back the heavy velvet curtain. It takes a moment for my brain to communicate with my eyes and process what I'm looking at. Standing in front of me, in all her glory, is Charlie smiling like a Cheshire Cat. I am so shocked to see her that I almost forget she is real.

"Hey babe," she says in her cool accent.

"Oh my God Charlie what are you doing here?" I splutter.

"Your fabulously gorgeous boyfriend got me here for a wee shopping spree. He's fucking amazing by the way. I'm your bra today honey," she laughs.

"This is so cool, and yeah he is rather amazing, but Charlie is he really my boyfriend?"

"Eh, excuse me? Are you kidding me?"

"It's just that neither of us ever asked each other out we just happened to, I don't know, be. We haven't even been on a date yet."

"There's a simple way to know if he's your boyfriend. Do you like him?"

"Yes."

"Do you get a little flutter in your belly when you see him?"

"Yes."

"Is he good to you, does he take care of you?"

"Yes."

"Have you had amazing, mind blowing sex?"

"Well, yes. My God yes."

She smiles and holds up her thumb. "Then he's your boyfriend. Now let's find Carolina I want to shop. Mark has given me free reign with his credit card and I intend to max it out."

"You go and find her while I read the rest of this note."

"Ooh bet there's some right dirty stuff for you to do in there." She winks at me and laughs. I roll my eyes at her and as she leaves, I open the note again and read the rest.

2. We are going out tonight. Charlie and Mark are joining us for dinner and drinks.

The dress code is smart casual. Underwear is optional.

3. After you have shopped you will be taken to a spa. Have whatever treatments you like.

4. Hairdressers next.

You have a driver for the day. When you are done shopping call the number on the card enclosed and you will be driven to your next destination. Your driver will collect you at 8pm sharp for dinner.

Take care and have fun.

Sx

I slouch back on the massive sofa. A driver for the day. Good God I feel like an actress or a pop star or something. Charlie is going to be in her element.

"Right doll face." Charlie's voice startles me. "Let's get shopping."

"Yes lets." I smile at her. This is going to be fun.

CHAPTER 24

"GINA THAT WAS THE single best shopping experience I have ever had." Charlie sighs as she throws her head back against the headrest of the Bentley.

"Your Boyfriend is an amazing piece of work by the way."

I have to agree with her. We shopped our little hearts out. Both getting gorgeous outfits for this evening. Charlie managed to find a really beautiful nude coloured chiffon and lace swing dress. I went for champagne coloured Capri pants and a black layered top with a black and white dogtooth jacket.

"Yeah I had fun too but I'm a little pissed that they wouldn't let us pay."

It turns out the *'spend as much as you like'* didn't apply to me spending as much of my own money as I liked only Steven's and that included Charlie. I was told by the cashier that the goods were already paid for and when Charlie tried to pay, she was told the same thing. I will have to speak to Steven about that. I know he is loaded but I like to pay my own way.

"Oh Gina come on it's not that bad! Don't you think it is great we have guys who want to spoil us?"

"It's okay for you, Mark is your fiancé and the father of your child. I've not known Steven long enough to be comfortable with all that yet."

Charlie looks at me with a big grin on her face. "Oh shut up woman. You're practically living with him. For the love of God will you just let him buy you some clothes?"

Holding up my hands in an *'I surrender'* gesture I say: "Okay, okay. I'll let it go this time just for you."

"Good girl. What are we doing next?"

"Well apparently, we have this driver for the day. I don't even know your name sir," I say to the salt and pepper haired man in the chauffer outfit.

"Name's Gerry ma'am."

"Nice to meet you Gerry. I'm Gina and this is Charlie."

"Lovely to make your acquaintance ladies."

Charlie looks at me and winks. "So is this your car

Gerry? It's really nice."

"No this is Mr Parker's car ma'am. I would love to own a car like this, but I can settle for driving it."

Steven's car! As well as the Aston Martin?

"Do you work for Steven Gerry?" I ask, my voice rather high pitched.

"I do. Have done for a while now."

I sink back into the seat. Wow, he must be really well off. Stunning cars, stunning apartment and employees.

"Right then ladies I have instructions to take you to a spa. Ready?"

Charlie looks at me with wide eyes. "Oh God yes Gerry. Gina, this guy is a keeper. He must have been a woman in a past life. Shopping and a spa... he knows how to treat a woman."

"We're going to a hairdressers after that too." I smile at her and her face breaks into a massive grin.

"Oh...I'm in heaven." She squeals and grabs my arm. "In all seriousness Gina I think he's been good for you. After all, if it weren't for him, you would never have called me. You would still be in mourning like Queen Victoria."

"I know Charlie, he's a great guy, I just don't know what he's doing with me."

Charlie turns to me and smacks me hard across the top of my arm.

"Ooow! What was that for?"

"Get a bloody grip Gina. You're a catch and if he can't see that then...I'll take him." She giggles at herself and I can't help but join in.

"Just accept it for what it is Gina, how everyone else sees it, he obviously really likes you. If it works out great, get married, have babies and grow old together. If it doesn't, well hey, at least you got back out there. You're still young, don't write yourself off now or you'll end up being a lonely old cat lady."

"I hate cats," I say with a smile. I know she's right it's just hard to imagine why someone like him would want someone like me.

"Well there you go then, a man yes, a cat no."

We pull up outside a lovely sandstone building.

"Oh Gina I've always wanted to come here. They have one of these hotels in Edinburgh too, the spa is the stuff of legend."

Gerry opens my door: "Right ladies, enjoy your afternoon. I'll be right here. Just let reception know when you are done and I will come in and escort you out."

Charlie starts to open her door and is scolded by Gerry. "Just you wait a minute Miss, I'll be right with you."

She flashes me a beaming smile; she's enjoying being pampered. I should be too, but I can't shake this nagging feeling that my happy little bubble could burst at any minute leaving me in tatters yet again.

"Thank you Gerry, you're such a gentleman," Charlie says in her poshest voice.

"You're welcome ma'am."

"Right toots let's get in and get pampered. I'm looking forward to a sleep on the massage table," Charlie says as she heads through the door leaving me in her wake.

***

"Oh my God Gina! I think I've had an out of body experience today." Sighs Charlie as we sit in the back of the Bentley.

Shopping, a spa and a visit to the hairdressers... what more could a girl ask for?

"As much as I hate to admit it Charlie this has been one amazing day. It's been even better because you're here with me." I feel tears threaten but I manage to hold them back.

"And why would you hate to admit it? Am I going to have to use physical violence to get you to bloody stop putting yourself down?"

"Sorry I'm pathetic I know, I just..."

"You just think that if you let yourself be happy something bad will happen."

"Yes. I know it won't, but it doesn't stop me from

thinking that way. Maybe it'll pass with time. This is all new to me. I was with Aiden for so long. The first time Steven touched me I felt like a bloody teenage virgin again."

As Charlie's eyes widen, I realise that I may have said that a little too loud.

"Oh God, sorry Gerry," I say as my face turns a lovely shade of pink. Gerry doesn't flinch. His eyes are fixed on the road.

"Gerry?" I say a little louder and look at Charlie

"Gerry?" She shouts and taps him on the shoulder. He reaches up to his right ear and removes a little flesh coloured bud.

"Yes ma'am?" He glances at Charlie in the rear-view mirror.

"What's that?"

She asks pointing to the mysterious little earplug.

"They are Bluetooth earphones. I thought you would like a little privacy so I'm listening to some music. Is there something I can do for you?"

I breathe an inward sigh of relief.

"No it's nothing, we were just wondering what you are doing tonight? When you are finished carting us around Glasgow I mean."

"Well, after you two ladies are ready, I'll take you to the restaurant and then I'll be heading out to have dinner with my girlfriend and my daughter."

"We'll be as quick as we can. Aren't you popular with the ladies today?" Charlie winks at him.

"Wouldn't have it any other way." He smiles back at her.

"That's us here ladies," he says as the car pulls up to Steven's building.

"Mr Parker asked me to give you this."

It is a little black box tied with a black ribbon.

Eyeing it suspiciously I carefully open it. Inside, sitting on a black velvet cushion, are two keys and an alarm fob attached to a key ring with the letter G attached to it. My breath hitches in my throat as I realise this is my set of keys for Stevens house. I need to be able to come and go for a few days but the spare set I used this morning would have done just fine. I don't think I can accept this.

Sensing my concern Charlie pipes up: "Thanks Gerry, we won't be long."

We get out the car before Gerry has a chance to help us grabbing our shopping as we go. He gives us a mock salute. As soon as we are inside the entrance Charlie grabs my hand.

"Breathe Gina. Are you okay?"

I shake my head. "I don't know Charlie. This all seems too fast. Why did he have to do this?" I say holding up the box. "Why couldn't he have spoken to me about it? I feel like I am being railroaded."

Charlie slaps her hand against her forehead and drags it down her face. "I swear to God Gina if you don't start listening to me, I am going to hit you and start charging you for therapy. I get it that Aiden was your life for so long and you feel like you are betraying his memory and blah blah blah, but you need to get it into that thick skull of yours that you have someone else now. Someone who really cares for you and may even be in love with you. I can't stand back and watch you throw it all away. He's gone Gina and the sooner you come to terms with that the better for all concerned. You have got to get over him."

Patting her growing belly she looks me straight in the eye with a hint of a tear in hers. "I need my friend right now. I'm so happy for you do you know that? I already told you I'm thankful to Steven for coming into your life because he brought you back into mine."

"Oh Charlie I'm so sorry." I sob and grab her and we cry on each other for a few minutes until Charlie lets out a loud snort and a laugh. Within seconds both of us are laughing and crying at the same time.

When we finally calm down Charlie looks at me and shakes her head. "What am I going to do with you my lovely?"

"Just bear with me Charlie I'll get there. I don't

know how but I will, I promise."

"Oh thank the lord. Now can we go and get these gorgeous clothes on? I can feel this baby getting bigger with every passing minute and I still want to fit into them when we get to dinner. My God I am starving. Wonder where we are going. Gina this place is stunning by the way; I can't believe you're actually living here. Gina. Gina. Earth to Gina." Charlie is waving her hand in front of my face and I realise that I have stopped at the top of the stairs.

"What the hell is up now?" She is starting to sound irritated.

"Sorry I got lost in my own head there. I just realised something."

"What?" She cocks her head to one side like an inquisitive little puppy. It makes me smile.

"Steven and I haven't been on a date yet. This will be our first official date."

"Eeeeeh Gina we need to get you dolled up to the nines." Charlie squeals with delight.

"No smart casual Charlie, not dolled up to the nines."

"Smart casual my arse Gina. We've got to make them take one look at us and want to do us in the middle of the restaurant...with an audience."

And this is what I love about Charlie. She is always positive no matter what might be getting her down and she always sees a way to push on through. I wish I could be half the person she is; my life would be much simpler.

"Okay then let's get cracking, we've only got two hours. Eight o'clock sharp Steven said."

CHAPTER 25

GERRY WAS BANG ON time to collect us from the apartment at eight. We were ready just in time. We definitely looked the part, dolled up to the nines didn't even come close. Charlie had done wonders with her make-up brushes and I had to admit that we looked awesome. If those men don't fall at our feet tonight, then they don't deserve us.

Gerry dropped us off outside a building on Great Western Road in the West End and pointed us in the direction of a black door. He handed me what looked like a credit card. It's matte black with only the address in the bottom right hand corner. Turning it over in my hand I wonder what it is for. Above the black door is a long black rectangle, again, with nothing written on it. It all seems very mysterious.

"Gina what the hell is this place?" Charlie whispers as she grabs my arm.

"I thought we were going to a restaurant; this place is creepy."

"I know. I never even knew this was here. It looks just like all the other buildings in the street. Let's get inside though, my feet are starting to get cold."

I try to open the door and find it is locked. I give it another push and then try with my shoulder. Still no luck.

"Look Gina," Charlie says pointing to a black metal object with a slit right down the middle. "Do you think that card will work in there?"

"Good grief, could Gerry not have told us that?"

I swipe the card down the slot and the door opens. There is an air of anticipation as we walk into a wide hallway decked out in black. The only hint of light comes from the twinkly LED lights in the ceiling and the quartz dotted through the shiny black tiles on the floor. Two large black sofas sit along one wall and at the end of the hallway is a reception desk with a woman standing behind it.

"Welcome to Black, may I take your card?" She is very slender and elegant and is wearing a plain black shift dress. Her hair is so black it almost looks blue under the lights. I look at her bemused.

"The card you used to gain access." She holds out her hand.

"Oh sorry." I laugh nervously, handing her the card. Swiping it through the card reader a look of realisation registers on her face. Her demeanour changes ever so slightly as her back straightens and her smile becomes more genuine.

"Ah…Ms Connor, Miss Olsson. Mr Parker and Mr Adams are expecting you. My name is Julie, if you would like to follow me."

Charlie nudges me and whispers: "Swanky."

Julie gives our jackets to the cloakroom attendant and we follow her through a set of black double doors. The sight that greets us on the other side is nothing short of spectacular. The dining area is completely black broken up by crisp white table cloths and sparkling silver candelabra. There are twenty or so round tables in the middle of the room with four booths along either side. Most of the tables are full. This is a busy place considering how inconspicuous it is. At the far end of the room is a dance floor, surrounded by strips of white LED lights, with a stage behind it. On the stage stands a black grand piano. A vast array of Champagne bottles are visible from the highly polished bar and crystal chandeliers complete the look of elegance. This place is stunning and I am so glad we made an extra effort tonight.

"Mr Parker and Mr Adams are in our VIP booth."

'Our VIP Booth' suggests that there is only one. Steven must have hired it out for this evening. As she leads us to the other end of the room, I spot the VIP booth. The round table is flanked on either side by two semi-circular booths. It could easily sit twelve people and is situated right next to the dance floor. Steven and Mark stand to greet us and I see my friend has done really well for herself. Mark is very good looking with thick dark hair and dark eyes. Their child will be gorgeous with that gene pool.

"Thanks Julie that will be all."

He must come here a lot to know the staff by name. Julie gazes up at him through her thick lashes and I get a horrible pang of jealousy. Is she is trying to flirt with him? She turns and sashays away. I don't like her.

"Hey gorgeous," Steven says, and I melt. He pulls me in for a slow, lingering kiss and whispers against my lips.

"You look fucking hot Gina, were there not an audience I would do you right here."

I can't help myself but laugh thinking of Charlie's words from earlier.

"What's so funny? Do you think I am kidding?"

"Sorry I'll tell you later. Thanks, you don't look

half bad yourself handsome."

He is wearing a charcoal grey suit and white shirt and no tie with the top couple of buttons undone. Now, that is sexy smart casual at its best. I turn to Mark and introduce myself.

"Hi there Mark, I'm Gina." I hold out my hand for a handshake but instead find myself encircled in a bear hug.

"I know who you are Gina. You're the person who has put the sparkle back into my girl's eyes."

As he releases me, I blush a little.

"I think we're both very glad to be in touch again. Congratulations on the baby, by the way, and thank you for naming her after me. I'm honoured."

Behind me I hear Steven clear his throat. "Anyone ready for dinner?"

"Absolutely," says Charlie. "I've been saving myself for this."

I am smiling from ear to ear as I look at everyone and think to myself that maybe there is a glimmer of hope that Steven and I could make this work and I can finally move on. As we take our seats Steven beckons a waiter.

"Good evening Mr Parker." The waiter is dressed in black and is carrying a tablet.

"Good evening James, we'll have a bottle of Cristal for the table please and what would you like

Charlie?"

"I'll have a virgin Pina Colada please James," says Charlie winking at him.

"Very good ma'am. Your food will be here shortly and I will have Lena bring your drinks."

James turns to Steven and with a little bow of his head says: "Sir."

He backs away from the table two steps before turning away.

"Do you come here a lot?" I ask Steven. "The staff seem to know you quite well."

He smiles at me. "They should know me well I pay their wages after all."

"That's a bit arrogant Steven. Just because you come here a lot doesn't mean you own them or anything." I glance at Charlie who is trying very hard to stifle a laugh.

"What?" I ask a little irritated.

"Think about it again honey."

"Oooooooh. Is this your club?"

Steven smiles and nods.

"You own this?"

"Still having those Joey moments darlin'?" Coos Charlie harking back to our Friends obsession days. I hold my hands up in mock defeat.

"Yes I am an idiot sometimes, but that's just one of the many things you love about me Charlie

Barley."

"Yes it is, wouldn't have you any other way babe."

She winks at me and I turn to Steven.

"So what exactly is this place?"

"It's a private members club. You can eat, drink and dance the night away all in one place." He talks about it with pride.

"You never told me you owned a club and, by the way, it's stunning."

"I agree," says Charlie. "It's like one of those places pop stars or footballers and their WAG's go."

"It is actually. We've had many celebrities here. Although there is a membership fee for most people, some celebs come on a one off if they're in Glasgow doing a concert or a play or something. They pay a premium for the privilege, though, this is one of the most exclusive clubs in Glasgow."

I listen, a little in awe as the waitress brings the drinks to the table. She is young, maybe early twenties, and like Julie has black hair pulled back into a high sleek pony tail. I wonder if black hair is a prerequisite to work here.

"Your drinks Mr Parker."

She has a thick South African accent and Charlie's head snaps up.

"Oh my God where are you from?"

She butts in before Steven can even thank the girl.

"Sorry."

Charlie says looking at Steven who regards her with amusement.

"Pretoria."

The waitress answers looking a little embarrassed having been ambushed by hurricane Charlie.

"I'm from Jo'burg, well I was born here but I lived there for years. I'm sorry but it is so nice to meet someone else from South Africa. I've been here so long and I don't get back much."

Oh my goodness Charlie is actually blushing. I didn't think anything could phase her.

"It's not a problem, I know what you mean. I get homesick too." She smiles at Charlie then turns to Steven. "Will that be all Sir?"

"Yes Lena, thanks."

"Very good."

Lena mimics James as she leaves. I wonder if everyone gets the star treatment or if it's just the big boss man. For some reason watching him wield power over people is a major turn on. As Lena leaves, James returns with the food as Steven explains: "We have a set menu each night. I have three award-winning chefs and they came up with the idea of offering classic cuisine from around the world. Tonight we are sampling dishes from Thailand."

"Ooh Charlie likes Thai right now don't you babe?" Mark says smiling at Charlie.

"I sure do but it is Georgie's fault not mine, she's feisty so she gets what she wants."

"Just like her mummy." Mark pulls Charlie in to his side and kisses her on the head, inhaling her scent as he does. They are such a gorgeous couple and I can see that Charlie is truly happy with Mark.

The food is astonishingly good. It reminds me of Spanish tapas with lots of small dishes, full of exotic smells and flavours. The conversation flows easily as though we have all known each other for years. Charlie and I reminisce about Uni while the boys chat about rugby and motor racing. Lena returns to refill our drinks.

"Will that be all sir?"

"Yes Lena, thank you. Are you due a break now?"

"Not for another five minutes sir."

"Why don't you take your break now? Sit and chat with Charlie and Mark here. I would like to show Gina some more of the club if you don't mind folks," he says to Charlie and Mark.

"Not at all, come and sit down Lena let's have a wee chin wag."

I love it when Charlie uses Scottish words in her funny Scottish tinged South African accent.

"Shall we Gina?" Steven says standing.

"Have fun you two and don't get lost." Charlie winks at us.

"We won't be too long," Steven says to them as he leads me away from the table.

Hand in hand we make our way towards a door to the right of the stage. Steven pulls out a black card and holds it in front of an almost invisible panel next to the door. The lock clicks and the door opens. The other side of the door is nearly identical to the hallway Charlie and I entered earlier. At the end of the hallway is another door, which opens up into a plush office. The industrial black steel coffee table in the middle of the room sits in stark contrast to the soft black sofas flanking either side. A solitary black laptop sits on the desk at the far side of the office. The only hint of colour in the room comes from a painting on the wall behind the desk. I recognise the style of the artist but I'm not familiar with this painting. It's of a man and a woman. She is pinned against the wall, arms raised above her head and legs slightly parted. His hand is between her thighs and you can see she is turned on, I can almost hear her moan. It is very erotic, almost pornographic and I can feel myself becoming aroused just looking at it.

"Is that a Vettriano?"

"Sure is, do you like it?"

"It's... different."

I'm mesmerised by it. The subject matter is extremely provocative. I move closer to have a better look.

"It's called 'Game On'. Unfortunately it's only a print. The original is in someone's private collection. I would love to get my hands on that."

As he says this, he moves quickly towards me and pushes me against the wall, pulls my arms above my head and thrusts the other between my legs. God this is hot. He kisses my cheek and down my neck while rubbing his hand over the seam of my trousers. Closing my eyes I enjoy this erotic moment and marvel at the way he can disarm me with his touch.

"Steven, we can't not here."

I am a little breathless and very turned on, but we can't do this here while Charlie and Mark are waiting for us back at the table.

"Says who?" He pulls me in close. "I can't keep my hands off you Gina," he whispers close to my ear. The warmth of his breath sends tingles all over my skin and I am about to give in when the office door flies open. My eyes fall on the blonde standing in the doorway. She is out of breath and has a manic look on her face. Her dishevelled look is in stark contrast to the clean, crisp surroundings Steven moves away from me and turns towards the doorway fixing her with an icy stare.

"How the fuck did you get in here Cheryl?"

Julie, from the front reception desk, appears behind her looking like a deer caught in headlights. "I'm so sorry Mr Parker, she bolted from me when I was trying to buzz through to you."

"It's okay Julie, can you take Gina back to the table please?" He moves away from me completely and I can tell he has closed me off.

"Steven what is going on here, who is she?"

"Julie, please," he says again avoiding me. I have no idea what is going on here but if he thinks I am going to hang around while he treats me like shit he is in for a shock.

"Don't bother Julie I can find my own way out," I say with venom in my voice.

"He's all yours," I say to Cheryl as I pass her. She looks older than I thought at first with dirty hair and well-worn clothes. Her teeth are all crooked and dirty and she's dressed like a hooker. She laughs as I run from the office and head down the corridor.

"Ms Connor wait." Julie calls after me. I stop and turn. The poor girl is flustered and looks embarrassed. "Ms Connor, I'm so sorry about that. She pushed past me and I couldn't stop her. She's stronger than she looks."

I hold my hand up to stop her. "Just tell me who she is." My voice is shaking.

"I'm sorry, I don't know who she is. You'll need to speak to Mr Parker about that." She looks genuinely remorseful. I decide to change direction.

"Tell me something Julie, how well do you know Steven?"

She looks a little flustered at my question. "Eh, well I've worked here for almost two years, but I wouldn't say I know him all that well. Why do you ask?" She says a little defensively.

"I'm not insinuating anything. I need to speak to someone who knows him well."

I can feel my cheeks redden and I sense tears bubbling under the surface. She looks at me with empathy, closes her eyes and takes a deep breath. When she opens her eyes again, she pulls out her phone and starts flicking through her contacts.

"I'm going to give you Steven's assistant's number. She's worked for him for a long time. Don't tell him that you got this from me, I need this job and I can't afford to lose it."

I give her my number and she sends me the contact details. "Why are you doing this?"

"Listen, I don't know him like a best friend but I'm not stupid. For the last two weeks he's been walking around with a smile on his face. An actual smile too, not the fake one he uses to schmooze the clientele. Even the way he's been talking to the staff is different." She smiles at me and nods her head. "I put it all down to you. Talk to Cerys, she may be able to help you. "

She gives me a shy smile then says: "And by the way I am a tad jealous that you snagged him. He's a handsome son of a bitch, isn't he?"

I smile back at her. He's more than handsome, he's every woman's dream. And therein lies my concern. He *is* every woman's dream so what the hell would he want with me? What's so special about me when he could have anyone he wanted? I need to talk to Cerys.

Stopping just inside the doorway I see Charlie and Mark sitting at the table. He has his hand on her bump, his head down talking to it and Charlie is laughing and looking at him with so much love in her eyes. She says something to him and he raises his head and kisses her. So soft and full of love, it makes my eyes sting. I burst into tears. I used to look like that, I used to be happy like that. I need to get out of here. I take long strides to the table and put on my best happy mask.

"Hey guys." I smile at them.

"Christ Gina, we were about to send out search and rescue to find you. Where's Steven?"

"Oh he has some business to deal with. Do you want to head back to the apartment? He'll follow on when he's done."

"Thank God, I need to get out of these shoes, my feet are aching. Lead the way darling." Charlie smiles at me as Mark stands to help her up. I grab my bag and pull out my phone. The message from Julie is showing on my screen. Ignoring it for the time being I send a text to Steven.

'We are leaving now. I'll see you back at the apartment. Explanation required.'

Pressing send I put the phone back in my bag. I give Julie a little smile as we pass her at the front desk then we head out into the cold dark night. I think I might like her now.

CHAPTER 26

WAKING FROM A RESTLESS sleep I squint my eyes in the dawn light peeking through the curtains. I had a myriad of strange and upsetting dreams and I feel awful. Charlie and I sat up chatting into the wee small hours. I told her everything that happened with Steven and his dad and the strange things that have been happening to me. By the time we went to bed at around 3am Steven was still not back. I tried to contact him but got no reply. I grab my phone from the bedside table and the time flashes up as 07.48 but there are no messages. My heart sinks. How can he do this to me after I pleaded with him to stop keeping me in the dark? I try again:

'Where on earth are you? I'm worried.'

Placing my phone on the table I head for the bathroom to brush my teeth. Just as I reach the door I hear the ping of a text message and bolt back to the bed. It is from Steven. I feel a tear escape. At last he has answered me.

'I'm in the kitchen.'

He's at home! Abandoning my teeth I run out of the bedroom taking the stairs two at a time and head straight for the kitchen. I stop at the door. He is sitting at the breakfast table with a load of paperwork in front of him and a cup of coffee in his hand. He is still wearing the clothes he had on last night. I can't help myself, I let out a little sob.

"Hey baby don't cry," he says as he gets up and walks over to me. "Everything is fine, I'm sorry I didn't call last night. I will explain." He wraps me up in his arms and I just let it all go.

"Steven you can't just disappear on me like that. It bloody scares me, especially with everything that's been going on."

"I'm sorry. Come, sit down and have some coffee and I'll explain everything." He pours me a coffee as I sit down.

"What time did you come home at?"

"About 2 hours ago. It was an interesting night I have to say." He cocks his head to the side and gives me a little half smile.

"Who was that woman last night Steven? She looked like a bloody prostitute."

"She is."

His answer floors me. "What the hell Steven? Why was a hooker in your club and how do you know her in the first place?"

"Cheryl is my dad's ex-wife. "

He shakes his head and sighs. "About two years ago, when I really started to make a name for myself, she started harassing me. It was just small things at first like silent phone calls, turning up at my office, just generally making a nuisance of herself. She blamed me for her marriage to my dad breaking up."

"But you were a baby for God sake, that wasn't your fault."

"Yes, I know that, you know that, and she gets it now. She lost everything when he left. She got into debt, got in with the wrong people, started taking drugs and turned to prostitution to fund her habit. It was one of those vicious cycles and she couldn't get out."

"So what does that have to do with you now? Why is she still hanging around?"

"Gina am I going to have to kiss you to finish this story or will you be quiet and let me go on?" He smiles that wicked little smile and I back down.

"Okay. So the last straw came when she broke into my office a few months ago. I didn't prosecute her because she didn't take anything or actually damage anything. I did, however, get to the bottom of what was going on. She said she was jealous that I had made all this money in spite of what my father had done and she felt that she deserved some too. She blamed me to an extent because it was when I came to live with them that their marriage broke down."

I go to speak and he holds up his hand.

"Ah ah ah no. I said she did blame me not that she still does. Obviously, I didn't have anything to do with it; I was just the product of the affair. Anyway, I made a deal with her that I would pay for her to go to rehab and help her back into work if she promised to get clean and stay clean."

"You're a good man Steven. Not many people would be prepared to help someone who despised them. I don't think I would."

"She lasted a week before she walked. She cleared out her bank account and then tried to get more money out of me. She came by the club as high as a kite and I told her if I saw her again, I would have her arrested and prosecuted for harassment. I didn't see her again until last night."

He gets up from his seat. "Want a re-fill?"

"Yes please," I say handing him my now empty

265

mug.

"I wanted to bloody punch her last night. Her timing couldn't have been worse."

I snort. "You don't say."

"Yes I know. However, she was there was to warn me."

"Warn you about what?"

"That bastard sent her a threatening letter telling her he was going to get her and beat her up like he did to all those other hookers and that he was going to make sure I always watched my back. She brought me the letter last night to show me."

As he comes back to the table, I take my coffee with shaky hands and even though it is hot I take a big gulp.

"Gina you don't have to worry," he says taking my cup and placing it on the table. He kneels at my feet and takes my hands in his.

"I went straight to the police with it as soon as I had made sure Cheryl was safe. She won't be bothering me again, but she says this has given her a wakeup call and that she'll be getting help. I knew you were safe; I tracked your phone until I knew you were back here. I also knew Charlie and Mark were with you. He's still in London and by now will be savouring the delights of her Majesty's displeasure. Sending that letter was a breach of his licence conditions and means an automatic re-arrest and imprisonment. Hopefully this time they will realise how dangerous he is and keep him locked up for good."

The feeling of relief that washes over me is huge. Knowing that Steven is safe from that monster is the best news I could hear. "Thank God Steven. I was so worried about you. I could never bear it if anything happened to you." I let out a sob and Steven pulls me off the chair and onto his lap on the floor.

"It's okay baby don't cry. I'm not going anywhere I promise." He holds my head on his shoulder. I feel safe with Steven. I know he means it when he says he isn't going anywhere but always, in the back of my mind, there is a niggling feeling that nothing is certain in this life. I've learned that the hard way. It just seems that every time we make some progress something always gets in the way. Hearing footsteps I look up and see Charlie standing in the doorway of the kitchen.

"Oh sorry folks. Is everything okay?" She can't hide the concern in her voice and she flashes Steven an 'I have my eye on you pal' look.

"Yes, lovely," I say plastering a smile on my face.

"I'll let Steven tell you all about it I need to go for a shower." I get up from the floor and wipe my hands over my tear stained cheeks. Charlie narrows her eyes

267

at me as if to say, 'I don't really believe you' and I smile a little wider.

"Honestly honey these are tears of relief." I kiss Steven on the top of the head and as I pass Charlie, I hug her and pat her bump.

"Now I am off to get cleaned up, I won't be long."

As I walk from the kitchen I'm filled with a renewed sense of purpose. All the drama of the last few days has certainly given me a lot to think about. When I get to the bedroom, I grab my phone and tap out a text to mum.

'Hey mum. I could do with your help flat hunting today. You up for it? Gx'

Laying my phone back on the bedside table I head for the shower. I need to wash off this yucky feeling. It might clear my head.

As I step under the hot steaming spray of the shower and let the warm water run over me, I feel my body relax. Leaning my head against the wall and closing my eyes, I block out all my thoughts and simply listen to the water falling around me. I wash with Steven's shower gel; the lemony smell is cleansing and invigorating. Taking my time to simply enjoy the feeling of tranquillity that has been so lacking in my life for so long. I like smelling like him. As I finish washing my hair, I get the feeling

268

someone is watching me. I turn and clear the glass with my hand and see Steven standing in the doorway, his shoulder against the frame. As he walks towards the shower, I get goose bumps. He strips off his clothes and steps in behind me and pulls my body in to his. He nuzzles his face into my neck.

"I'm so sorry baby." He whispers. I turn in his arms and kiss him softly as the water pours over us. There is nothing rushed or frenzied about this. He lifts me slowly off my feet and I wrap my legs round his waist. The running water making it very easy for me to slide down on to him. He presses us against the wall under the hot stream. Our movements are minimal and so intimate as if we are one person. I feel his back muscles tense and I know he is as close to orgasm as I am. We both come together. He holds me for the longest time as the hot water runs over us. I don't want to ever lose this feeling of closeness and love.

CHAPTER 27

CHARLIE AND MARK LEFT at lunchtime to head back to Edinburgh. It was fun seeing Charlie's face when Gerry pulled up outside in the Bentley to give them a ride home. She squealed with delight and gave Steven a huge hug. Mark was a little more laid back and shook his hand. After they had gone Steven headed off to the office and I went to meet mum. I had made several appointments with estate agents to look at apartments in the city centre. We went to see five different ones in all in different parts of the city. Ideally, I would have liked one close to Steven, however, the West End is a little out of my price range. I found two in the Merchant City area that are stunning. I need to make a decision and get things moving before Christmas. We stop off at a little coffee shop in the Italian Centre, where one of the two flats is situated. The place is festooned with Christmas decorations and is cosy and welcoming. I can see myself living here among the designer shops and city nightlife.

"Thanks for today mum. I feel a million times better now that I know where my life is going and I am finally moving forward."

She reaches over and pats my hand. "Oh my darling I am so happy for you. That boy is a keeper. Your dad just loves him to bits."

My phone buzzes on the table and I see that Steven has sent me a text.

'Hey babe what would you like for dinner? I'm cooking.'

I smile as I text him back.

'Surprise me! x'

'You may live to regret that. See you later gorgeous. x'

"See," says mum. "Look at the smile on your face. I assume that's Steven?"

"Yes he's making dinner tonight. I have yet to see him cooking so this could be interesting."

"Right darling I'm going to have to love you and

leave you. Dad and I are meeting with Stan Mitchell and his new wife for dinner." She rolls her eyes as she talks about my solicitor and her ex colleague.

"His new wife, how many has he had?"

"Oh this is number five. I'm surprised he has any bloody money left the rate he goes through them," she laughs. "I just wonder how much younger this one is going to be."

"I'm meeting with him on Monday so don't go putting him in a bad mood. "

She makes a crisscross gesture over her chest: "Cross my heart, I promise."

"Right well I'll let you get on and I'll go and see what Gordon Ramsay's understudy is cooking up."

"Okay sweetheart, take care and let me know what you decide about the flats."

We stand, and hug and I give her a kiss on the cheek. "Love you mum. Enjoy your night."

"We will. Bye darling."

As she walks away, I stare at her retreating figure and think to myself how lucky I am to have both my parents. Poor Steven never had that luxury. Well he can share mine, they have more than enough love to go around. I pay for the coffees and head on out myself.

As I make my way through town, window shopping as I go, I feel happy and for the first time in a long time I don't feel guilty. It is a nice sensation. On Buchanan Street outside Princes Square I notice a few little kids and their parents. The children have brightly coloured balloons and are all dressed in warm coats and hats. They all dance around in a circle while their parents chat to each other and I think to myself what a lovely picture that would make. The children would be nice in black and white with the balloons in colour. I realise that I have not picked up my camera since Aiden died. I haven't wanted to. God, have I really not taken a single picture for six months? That can't be right. It's high time I started again, started really living and not just treading water. There are countless photo opportunities in this wonderful city and I am missing them all. As my camera is still at my own house, I decide now might be a good time for an upgrade, so I head over to Frasers to see what they have on offer.

I don't go overboard but I do leave the shop with my bank account almost three thousand pounds lighter. If money was absolutely no object that three thousand could easily have been quadrupled. The selection of cameras and equipment had me drooling. I decide to buy a gift for Steven as a thank you. He has helped me get my life back on track and I'm so glad he came into my life when he did. With my shopping all done I head out onto Argyle Street and hail a taxi. It's getting dark and my feet are on fire. As the taxi pulls up outside Steven's place, I notice his car parked outside and a huge smile spreads over my face. I notice a young woman sitting on the steps in front of the building. I stop and regard her for a second and she stands up. She has long dark brown hair and very pale skin. I notice that she is heavily pregnant and certainly not dressed for this weather in just a T-shirt and trousers and a pair of ballet pumps.

"Are you okay? You'll freeze out here in this weather."

She reaches into her back pocket and takes out her phone. Pointing it in my direction she takes a picture, the flash momentarily blinding me.

"What the hell are you doing?" I shout.

"Fuck you bitch!" She screams at me with venom in her voice and turns and runs to a waiting car. The car takes off at speed with the tyres screeching.

I can't move. I stand there with my mouth hanging open, dumbstruck. What was that? Is she Steven's ex? Is that his baby? My imagination is on overdrive. Oh God I can't take much more of this, I swear I am about to have a nervous breakdown. I don't know how but I manage to get upstairs and into the apartment and as soon as the door is closed, I collapse onto my knees in a mess. The smell of cooking, which should have me salivating, is making me feel sick.

"Gina is that you?" I hear Steven's voice coming from the kitchen. I can't even speak. My forehead rests on the cold tiles. I hear Steven come out of the kitchen and into the hall.

"Jesus Gina what's happened?" He is down on his knees by my side, but I can't even look at him. This is the last straw. I can't handle this anymore. I should have stayed where I was, pathetic little Gina, and lived the rest of my life on my own.

"Gina will you sit up and look at me please?" His voice is full of concern but all I really need is to get out of here quick. I sit back on my heels and swipe at my eyes.

"Steven please forgive me." I am hysterical and probably don't make much sense. "I can't do this anymore, I need to go. I'm so sorry."

As he reaches out to touch me, I jerk away. I put my head in my hands and rock back and forth saying over and over: "I'm so sorry, I'm so sorry, I'm so sorry."

"Gina will you tell me what the fuck has happened?" He sounds angry.

"I just can't do this Steven. I'm a fucking mess and I can't be here anymore. I can't be around you anymore, I can't be around all this anymore. Please, just leave me alone." I stand up on shaky legs. I can't look at him for fear I may give in. I open the door and walk out pulling it closed behind me.

I hear Steven shout 'FUCK IT' so loudly it startles me. That is followed by a massive smash and more expletives. I run down the stairs and out of the building. Somehow, I end up on the main road and hail a taxi. As soon as I have given the driver my address I sit back and sob the whole way home. My heart is completely broken and worse than that is the realisation that I have broken Steven's heart in the process.

CHAPTER 28

I LIE IN BED staring at the wall in the semi darkness with massive puffy eyes. It is very early on Sunday and day two post meltdown. I ripped the house phone out of the socket on Friday evening and fell into bed and the only time I have moved is to pee. I have not looked at my mobile, but I know Steven will have called. I still have on the same clothes I came home in on Friday and I haven't eaten a thing. I am exhausted and I know I must look an eyesore. My mirror doors still bear the lipstick writing and I don't even care anymore. I am an absolute wreck, a hollow empty shell of a person again, only this time it's worse. This time I did it to myself.

Every time I close my eyes, I see that woman and

the nasty look on her face. Why was she sitting outside Steven's house? Who was she? What does she mean to Steven? I feel myself start to drift off to sleep again but a creaking noise from downstairs startles me. I pull the duvet up to my chin my eyes bulging and my ears straining. There is another creaking noise, this time on the stairs. Oh my God, this is how I will meet my end, alone and with puffy eyes. I pull the duvet over my head and squeeze my eyes shut. There are footsteps on the top hallway and I hear my door opening. I will myself to wake up. I know this is not a dream when the duvet is pulled off me and a torch shone on my face. I put my hand up to shield my eyes and can just about make out the form of a female.

"Sit up." She whispers. I do as I am told and she flicks on the lamp on the bedside table. As the light fills the room, I am shocked to see that it is the woman from outside Steven's house.

"What do you want?" I ask, my voice shaking.

"Shut the fuck up bitch, you don't talk unless I tell you to right."

I notice a large carving knife in her hand. Oh God she does mean to kill me! What the hell have I done to her? I don't even know her. She can see the fear in my eyes and laughs at me.

"Aw what's wrong did the little rich boy chuck

you out? You didn't deserve all that anyway. You took my money. You took my baby's money," she says all this through gritted teeth and just when I think she is going to lift the knife and stab me she doubles over holding on to the edge of the bed dropping the knife on the floor. She grabs her belly as her pain contorts her. Holy crap this girl is in labour. What the hell do I do?

"Are you okay?"

"I ... said ... shut ... up." She takes in a massive breath.

"No you obviously need help. I don't care who you are let me help you."

When the contraction has passed, she lifts her head and looks at me. "Why the fuck would you want to help me? Are you stupid? Really?"

"No I'm not stupid I just think you need help. You need to be in hospital with people who are trained to help you and your baby."

"You really want to help me give me my money."

"I don't know what you're talking about. What money? I don't have any of Steven's money."

"Steven? Is that your rich boy's name? He's nothing to do with me. I don't know him."

I'm bloody confused. "Then how can I possibly have your money? I thought that was Steven's baby?"

She lets out a shrill laugh and just as she is about

to speak another contraction takes hold. "Aaaarrrrggg!" She screams so loudly it sounds like someone is being murdered. I am no doctor or midwife, but I know these contractions are coming close together and that is not a good thing. I jump down from the bed and put my hand on her back. She jumps slightly but allows me to rub it for her.

"How long have you been having these?"

"I don't know…a few hours," she says. Her forehead has a sheen of sweat over it and her cheeks are flushed.

"What's your name?"

She kneels on the floor and with her head resting on my bed. "Abby."

"Did you do this?" I say pointing to my mirrors. She nods and turns to look at me. Her eyes are wide and filled with tears. She looks like a scared little girl.

"Why? What did I ever do to you? I don't even know you."

She turns her head away again and starts mumbling something I can barely hear. It sounds like 'I loved him'.

"Loved who Abby? What are you talking about?"

As another contraction begins, she starts to cry. We need medical help here; I can't deal with this on my own.

"I need to call you an ambulance Abby, these

contractions are really close and that baby will be coming soon." I am getting scared now. I don't have a clue how to deliver a baby. I get up to go downstairs and get my phone, but she grabs my leg.

"No please don't leave me." She is in floods of tears now and I feel so bad for her.

"I'm just going to get my phone, I'll be right back."

She lets go and I race downstairs and grab my bag. Fumbling around for my phone I upend it and pour the contents all over the kitchen table. Before I locate the phone my key for Steven's apartment falls off the table. Looking at it lying on the floor I start to cry. Why did I do this to him? I am stupid she is right. I find my phone and as I do, I hear another scream from upstairs.

"Gina, help me please!"

"I'm here, I have my phone and I'm calling an ambulance."

The contraction passes as I reach the bedroom. She looks dreadful, but it is not a look of exhaustion it is one of sorrow and something else I can't quite put my finger on. I glance down at my phone as the screen lights up and there are over a hundred missed calls from Steven and the voicemail icon is going mental. My heart sinks at the thought of him trying to get in touch for hours on end. I call for an ambulance.

The operator tells me there is a crew close by and that they should be with us in ten minutes.

"I'm sorry Gina," she says with her head bowed.

"But why me and why do you keep saying I have your money?"

"Are you seriously telling me you don't get this by now?" She looks at me sceptically.

I stare back at her and as the realisation of her words start to filter in, I start to shake.

"No. No. No. This can't be right. Are you telling me...No!" I can't take this in.

"Yes Gina, this is Aiden's baby."

"NO NO NO NO!" My whole world has just been pulled out from under me and I am losing my grip on reality.

"You fucking bitch! You dirty fucking bitch!" I think I am about to pass out. Falling to my knees I scream: "Please help me! I can't take this anymore!"

"Oh God here comes another one." Abby grabs my hand and squeezes hard as the pain rips through her. Right now all I really want to do is punch her.

"Breathe Abby, just breathe through it." I tell her. As the contraction stops, she loosens her grip on my hand slightly and I pick up my phone. The operator on the line is fantastic and talks me through everything. First of all she gets me to time the contractions. We do three to determine how close she is and it appears that this baby may be coming in the next few minutes. I hope and pray that the paramedics get here before then.

"Oh Gina I need to push."

"Are you kidding me?"

I drop the phone and can hear the tinny squawk of the operator. Flicking the phone onto speaker I ask the operator what I need to do. Following her instructions I get Abby to strip from the waist down and get on all fours. Her contractions are coming fast now and lasting so long that I can't keep track of them anymore. I am willing the paramedics to arrive. The next few minutes pass in a blur. Before I know it, I am holding a tiny, crying, baby girl in my hands. All I can do is stare at her. The sound of footsteps stirs me into action and I wrap this poor wee baby up in a blanket.

"Abby the paramedics are here are you ok?" She doesn't answer me.

"Abby!" I shout to her. "Oh my God help us she's not moving!"

Two paramedics rush through the door. I lay the baby down and stand aside as they deal with the little one, cutting the cord and then tending to Abby herself. I sit down on the chair in my bedroom and watch the scene unfold. I am in a state of shock. I can't process what just happened.

Abby and her baby are taken to the hospital and as I close the door behind them the eerie silence engulfs me. I collapse in a heap on the floor wailing at the top of my voice: "How could you Aiden? How could you do this to me?" My sobs echo around the hallway. "You fucking bastard!"

I feel my hand vibrate and realise it's my phone; it's Steven.

"Gina?" I can hear him breathing. "I need to see you Gina, I miss you."

As I sit looking at my phone I can't speak. All I feel is betrayal and loss as I curl up into a ball on the floor. I can hear Steven's voice as sobs wrack my body and I finally pass out.

***

The door opens and I look up into a pair of bloodshot, red rimmed blue eyes. He has stubble on his face and his hair is a mess. He looks awful. He takes one look at me and collapses down beside me, pulling my limp body into his arms. He holds me for the longest time. He smells of whisky.

"Come home with me Gina, please?" He says, his voice almost a whisper and I nod my head. Home sounds good. This place is dead to me. As dead as the man I thought I knew. Steven carries me to the Bentley and Gerry opens the back door. Steven puts

284

me down on the seat and asks Gerry to collect some of my personal belongings and lock the door before joining me. As we drive away, I don't give the house a backward glance, instead I curl my body in to Steven's and cry.

CHAPTER 29

THE SOFT STRAINS OF a piano and violins emanate from the car speakers. I am snuggled in to Steven's side and every time I sob, he kisses my hair. It is the nicest, sweetest gesture. As we near Steven's apartment, having sat in silence the whole way there, he leans forward and taps Gerry on the shoulder.

"Yes?" Gerry says as he takes out one of his little ear buds.

"Gerry can you contact Cerys and ask her to hold all my calls?"

"Sure will, anything else?"

"No, thanks Gerry. Go home and get some rest, I won't need you for the rest of the day."

"Thanks."

I am still wearing my bloodied, ruined clothes and am barefoot. Steven lifts me out of the car, taking my bag from Gerry, and carries me in to the building. He sets me down in the entrance hallway and opens the door. As I follow him in, I am shocked at the scene that greets us. Broken pottery is scattered everywhere and the large picture from above the hall table is propped against the wall with the frame broken and the glass shattered into a thousand tiny shards. I gasp and cover my mouth with my hand. All the curtains are shut and it bloody smells.

"Sorry." Steven whispers.

I feel wretched. This was my doing, I made this happen. He looks at my bare feet and carries me through to the living room, depositing me on one of the sofas before stalking into the kitchen and emerging with a dustpan and brush.

"Steven leave it, I'll help you later." My throat is hoarse and my voice comes out all croaky.

"No, I need to fix this, need to fix it so you don't see it, I can't let you see it, can't let you see me like this." He is mumbling and I wonder if he is speaking to himself or me.

"Please just leave it..."

"NO." His raised voice startles me and his red rimmed eyes bore into my soul. He looks vulnerable. His usual 'I can handle the world' mask is gone and

287

all I see is a scared little boy. He looks away from me and continues out into the hall. I hear the clatter of pottery and glass. We need to talk but I don't know what to say. I don't know what to do to make this better. I fucked up beyond belief.

As my thoughts are warring with each other he walks back in to the living room. Without looking at me he heads to the kitchen.

"Drink?" He asks with his back to me. His words short and clipped. He's mad.

"I'll have whatever you're having."

When he emerges from the kitchen, he is carrying two glasses filled with amber liquid and a bottle of whisky. He bangs the whole lot down on the table and sits opposite me on the sofa, glass in hand. He sits staring at the window, at the closed curtains.

"Steven."

He takes a long drink of whisky.

"Steven look at me please."

"I can't, not yet Gina." He carries on staring at the window.

"Okay, will you let me explain?"

He shrugs. "Explain away."

"Steven I can't even begin to tell you how sorry I am. Sorry for everything. Sorry for..."

"Sorry for not letting me into your fucked up world?" He cuts me off and now he looks at me. His

288

eyes are full of dejection.

"Don't you dare Steven! You know how hard this has been for me and I'm sorry but I'm not the only one who's fucked up here. You basically spied on me for months, you went off at me because of your scumbag dad, you disappeared for days without so much as a text to let me know you were okay, you fraternise with hookers. Who's fucked up? I was just trying to get on with my life, I didn't ask for all this crap."

He stands up and fires his glass across the room. It smashes against the wall and shatters into tiny pieces. The amber whisky running down the white paint is grim. I put my head in my hands.

"I never asked to be married to a fucking cheating bastard and I certainly never asked to be held at knifepoint in my own home."

"What?" Steven says incredulously. "Knifepoint, what are you talking about Gina?"

"Oh... you don't know about that. For some stupid reason I thought that's why you called."

"Gina, I have been calling you almost every hour since you walked out of here. Now will you tell me what you are talking about?"

He sits beside me on the sofa and looks down at the T-shirt I am wearing, pulling at the hem. "Where did this blood come from, are you hurt?"

I pull it out of his hands and move away. "No I'm fine, well physically I'm fine."

I take as big a breath as my lungs will allow. "When I came back here on Friday, I was full of hope, feeling that I'd finally made the right decision about my future. I found a few apartments with mum and I was dying to come home and tell you. Thing is I got ambushed outside your building by this very heavily pregnant girl. She was so bloody nasty and I thought she had something to do with you. I thought her baby was probably yours."

His eyebrows almost shoot right off his forehead. "Mine? Jesus Gina you could have told me this on Friday."

"I didn't know what to think. I couldn't think clearly. That's why I left, to try and clear my head…to give me some space. I went home crawled into bed and that's where I've been until this morning."

He motions with a nod of his head to the TV room. "I've been holed up in there since Friday."

"I'm so sorry Steven, you have no idea. That fucking stupid girl turned up at my house with a fucking knife and then proceeds to go into full-blown labour. I swear to God you could not make this shit up."

"Who is she?" He asks as he leans forward and

290

gently tucks a few stray hairs behind my ear.

I snort a little and shake my head. "This is where it gets really fucked up. She was Aiden's mistress."

"And the baby?" He asks although he already knows the answer.

"His."

"That fucking prick. Don't you dare stick up for him Gina I mean it! He was a fucking prick." Steven starts pacing the floor. "What else did she tell you?"

"Well, she admitted she was the one who wrecked my bedroom and sent the email, but we didn't really talk all that much because I ended up delivering her baby." I pull at the hem of my T-shirt. "Hence the blood."

He looks at me and puts his hand to his forehead. "My God Gina..." He strides over to me and puts out his hand to me. I shake my head.

"Steven I'm sorry, I need some time to process all this. My head is all messed up. Can you give me some time?"

"I'll give you anything you need. Please just do one thing for me."

"What?"

"Will you stay here while you sort all this out?"

"I don't know Steven, I really need space. I was actually thinking about a hotel or something."

He puts his hand over his heart. "Gina, I promise,

you won't even know I am here. Please, just stay?"

"Okay."

"Thank you." Steven almost reaches out to hug me but stops himself. "Sorry, space. I forgot myself there. It won't happen again. I'll go and sort out a room for you and you can get yourself cleaned up okay."

"Thank you." He gives me a small smile, but it doesn't reach his eyes.

Getting up from the sofa, I lift the glass of whisky Steven poured for me and the bottle and head into the kitchen. I'm hungry and I'm going to drink what is left of this bottle, so I think it is probably best to eat something. The fridge is well stocked and I find a jar of olives and some mozzarella cheese. That will do nicely. I notice some pots and pans on the hob and realise this was probably Friday's dinner and could be partly responsible for the God-awful smell. My bag is sitting on one of the chairs at the table. I get my phone out and stick my earphones in. I put on the loudest mind-numbing dance music I can find, turn it up loud and sit down at the breakfast bar to eat and drink. The food is good, but the whisky is even better. It goes down with a burn and then leaves that smoky, warming aftertaste. I finish the first glass in one go and pour another. I've never had whisky for breakfast before.

I get off the bar stool, glass in hand and hold it up.

"Cheers to you Aiden you fucking man-whore bastard!" I shout over the music. I laugh hysterically at myself, finish the glass, and proceed to call him all sorts of other derogatory names.

"You monkey-shit, fuck-face, stupid dog-breath wanker."

I am starting to feel very sorry for myself. I loved that bastard and he took my heart and ripped it to shit. Pouring another glass and downing it in one, I start a crazy little dance to myself. After whirling round the kitchen looking like a mad woman, and almost knocking myself out because I lost my balance at one point, I decide maybe I should get showered and changed out of these clothes. I stink and my hair looks like it spent a week in a deep fat fryer. I pull out my earphones and put my phone away. My ears are ringing. Lifting my glass and the remainder of the bottle I walk back through to the living room and I notice that the whisky glass Steven threw at the wall has been cleared up. When did he do that? I didn't see him come into the kitchen Oh God did he see me acting like a total nut-case?

As I walk through the house and up the stairs it dawns on me that the place is empty. He's gone. I asked for some space, but I thought he would have said if he was going out. He's prepared a room at the

293

front of the apartment for me, as far away from his room as you can possibly get. Looking out the bedroom window I notice that his car is still parked out in front. I wonder where he has gone. Stripping off my clothes I dump the whole lot in the bathroom bin. There is no way in hell I am wearing them again. I turn on the shower and let it heat up and as I step under the hot stream, I feel tears welling in my eyes. Before I know it all my grief, hurt and anxiety comes flooding out. I sink to the floor. I know this is going to be a long road. I just wonder if my poor shattered soul is going to be strong enough cope with it.

CHAPTER 30

IN THE WEEK FOLLOWING my encounter with Abby I spend a lot of time flitting between sadness and anger. My heart has been utterly shattered; the last year of my life with Aiden seems like a joke. A cruel joke. I feel humiliated. Steven is true to his word and has given me space and let me come and go as I please. He has stayed out of my way and even though we have been in the same house for four days I have hardly seen him. He is gone when I wake and has only been back once before I have been asleep, even then I think that was an accident on his part. How I long to be with him again. Even to be within touching distance of him. I don't know how he feels about me. I fucked up badly when I ran out on him but for the time being, as long as he'll have me, I'll stay. I have promised myself I will make up for this.

I visited Abby in hospital two days after the baby was born. I needed answers. What happened that morning in my bedroom was traumatic, not just for me but also for Abby. I don't know if she intended to harm me or not. Grief can do strange things to a person's mind. It was one of the hardest things I have had to do and I was filled with a sense of dread as I walked into the hospital. I'm glad I went through with it. Abby had been bleeding internally after the baby, who she named Kayleigh, was born. She had gone into shock and that's why she was unresponsive. The paramedics had arrived just in time. If they had been any later, she may have died. I could never imagine that poor little soul growing up without a mother or a father. My thoughts immediately went to Steven. That's basically what happened to him, although he would probably have been better off without that man in his life at all.

Abby and Aiden met each other at a motorbike club that he belonged to. He used to go out with his mates once a month and they would ride their bikes, get dinner then ride home. Abby was at one of the meets last June with her brother. She and Aiden got talking and hit it off right away. They kept in touch and began to see each other more and more until their friendship changed. I asked her not to go into too much detail, but I did find out that they started sleeping together almost a year ago and she found out she was pregnant in March. He told her he would make sure I was out of the picture before the baby came but that he would make sure I did the leaving because he didn't want to be lumped with the guilt trip of breaking up with me. I swear right then I could have gladly vomited all over her hospital bed or punched her in the face. I felt sick to my stomach at what she was telling me. What he was planning to do was really nasty and the fact that she would have let him do that doesn't stand her on any moral high ground. I did nothing to deserve that. All I had ever done was love him. I realised then that this was what had prompted the argument that night, I just never thought for a moment that I was right when I asked him if he was having an affair.

Abby said she didn't know that he was married until she told him she was pregnant. I don't know whether that made me feel better or worse. She said if she had known about me, she would never have let it get that far. I have my reservations about that. Apparently, she only found out he had died two days after the accident when she read about it in the paper. She said she had come to the crematorium but stayed well back. She told me that she had been watching me for months. She would sit outside my house and follow me into town every Tuesday when I went for my appointments with Nate. I really wracked my brain trying to think why I had never seen her. She said that was how she had managed to find out where Steven lived. She decided to show herself that night because she knew she didn't have long to go until her baby came and she wanted to get some of Aiden's life insurance money to help care for her when she did arrive. So that was what that life insurance policy he had taken out without my knowledge was for and explained why there was no next of kin noted. She knew about it, so he had to have told her, little did she realise she would need it so soon.

We chatted a while longer and I cried, she cried, the baby cried. I couldn't really bring myself to hold her again. I just wanted to be out of there, but I did assure Abby that her daughter would be taken care of. I said I would arrange for some money to be transferred to help her get back on her feet but once that was gone, she was on her own. She didn't argue with that. I think she knew she was lucky to be getting anything at all from me. I owe her nothing. I told her that I never wanted to see or hear from her again. She agreed that would be for the best. I left the hospital that day with a heavy heart. I knew that all my guilt and internal turmoil over moving on with my life after Aiden had all been for nothing. I had put myself through hell for the last six months on the belief that I had lost the one man who loved me when really, he might as well have crushed my heart in his fist for all he actually cared for me in the end.

I went straight from the hospital to my appointment with Nate. I had called in the morning and asked Fiona if I could speak to him myself. When I explained what had happened and that I had planned on going to see Abby, Nate cleared two hours for me. My nerves were completely shot by the time I left the hospital and talking things through for an hour and a half was the best thing I could have done. Nate tried to reassure me that none of this was my fault. The only person to blame for all of this was Aiden. The one person I thought I could trust with my life was going to break my heart and make me think it was my doing. That was not the man I fell in love with and married. That man was not callous and cold, and he certainly would never have hurt me like that. Nate said that I will always have unanswered questions but what I should take from this is that I am still here with a life ahead of me and it is up to me what I chose to do with it.

The one other thing that I gleaned from that session was that Nate is more than just Steven's therapist, he's also his friend and he told me, off the record of course, that in the few weeks I have been with Steven he has never seen him so happy. He did, however, say that there are a lot of things I have yet to find out and that I need to be strong and take the bad with the good. What he meant by that I have no idea, but I do get the feeling that there is more to the relationship with Steven and his father than what he has told me.

After I had finished with Nate, I went to see mum and dad. It was hard telling them about Aiden and the affair. Seeing the heartbreak in my dad's eyes when I told him what he had been doing and what he planned to do all but destroyed him. My parents loved him like a son, my dad was the one who had introduced us. I don't think in my whole life I have ever seen my mum stuck for words but telling her about Aiden's affair and the fact that I basically delivered his baby more or less stopped her dead. I was gutted for them, and having to relive everything for a third time that day had me mentally and physically exhausted. Mum asked if I wanted to stay over but deep down, I just wanted to be near Steven and sleeping in one of his beds alone was as close as I could get to him. Just knowing that at some point he was there, even if I was sleeping, was solace enough.

By far, the worst thing I have had to do this week was to get in touch with Sandra. With everything that has gone on in the last few weeks I never got the chance to speak to her and let her explain about the message she left on my answering machine. It was with a heavy heart that I contacted her the day after I had been to see Abby. We chose to meet in a little coffee shop in the city centre yesterday. Somewhere neutral. What I had to tell her was going to be hard for her to hear.

***

I find Sandra with her head bowed staring into a mug of coffee.

"Sandra, thanks for meeting with me," I say putting my hand on her shoulder. She looks frail compared to the last time I saw her. She doesn't speak, only nods to me. Her eyes are watery and I immediately feel so sorry for her. I am about to make her day worse. I sit down opposite her and take her hand in mine.

"Sandra I am so sorry..."

"No Gina. I'm the one who is sorry. I can't believe I was so stupid to do that to you. I honestly don't know what came over me that day I called you."

"I was very hurt by what you said Sandra. You know I love you, I always have and it cut so deep when I heard that message. Tell me what I did that was so wrong."

She shakes her head, defeated. "I had been out shopping and sometimes, on my way home, I drive past your house. I don't know why, I think it comforts me. I saw the For Sale sign up outside and I just lost it Gina. It felt like I was losing Aiden all over again. I felt utterly disgusted with myself afterwards. It was made even worse when the police turned up at my door. What on earth happened Gina?"

Her eyes are sad and pleading and I feel terrible for her.

"Oh Sandra I don't even know where to start." I tell her about the break in and the email. It takes an enormous amount of courage to tell her about Abby.

"Sandra, I don't know how to tell you this." I take a deep breath and decide she needs to know the truth. She needs to know her son was not the angel she thought he was but more than that she needs to know she has a grandchild.

"Aiden was having an affair."

Her mouth drops open in disbelief. It takes a moment or two before she can speak. "How do you know?" She finally says.

"His mistress was the one who did those nasty things to me. She broke in to my house again and held a knife to me. She was pregnant Sandra." She holds her hand over her mouth as she shakes her head slowly.

"Are you okay?" I ask. I am worried about her.

"Oh Gina honey I am so sorry. What the hell was he thinking?"

"Sandra, I have made my peace with this. I'm moving on with my life. I don't know if you know or not, but I am seeing someone now and I will be moving to a new house as soon as I can."

"Who is she? If she's carrying my son's child, I have a right to know where I can find her."

"She's in the maternity unit at the Royal Infirmary. I helped her deliver her baby; she was in labour when she came to my house. She had that wee girl on my bedroom floor."

Poor Sandra looks like she is going to throw up.

"I can't apologise to you enough Gina. I didn't raise my children to behave like that. Oh God I can't believe he would do that. I'm so sorry, so very sorry Gina."

Tears fall from her eyes and I can't help but move to her side and hug her tight. "Please Sandra this was not your fault. I will give you Abby's contact details. You have a granddaughter and you should be involved in her life. I apologise to you now for what I am about to say. I love you with all my heart, but I can't be part of your family anymore. What Aiden did was despicable and I can't bear to be reminded of his betrayal every time I see you. I hate him. I gave him everything and it was as if it meant nothing to him. Please let me go and get on with my life and you have to do the same. I am sure Abby will be okay with you seeing the baby. You'll be a brilliant grandmother I know you will."

Sandra nods her head in acceptance and we both stand and hug each other. I give her a piece of paper with Abby's details on it and we part ways.

Walking out of the coffee shop with tears in my eyes, I don't look back. That chapter of my life is closed and I am so glad I got the chance to see Sandra again one last time. I hope something good can come of this horrible mess.

***

It's late Thursday evening now and I have been moping around this vast apartment by myself for the last four days. Yesterday, after my meeting with Sandra, I arranged to have all my belongings packed up and put into storage with the help of Charlie and Mark. Charlie tried to pretend she was calm and patient when I told her everything; however, the tone of her voice belied her fury. She and Mark dealt with everything so that I could wash my hands of the house. It's being sold furnished, I want nothing from it. My dad had my car taken to their house and I am getting rid of that too. I need to clear all the negativity out my life. Anything that reminds me of him has to go.

I go into the kitchen and pour myself a coffee popping my iPhone into the kitchen dock as I go. Having selected a random playlist I'm not sure what I'll get so when the first bars of a Sam Smith song start, I almost drop my mug. This song could have been written about me. I stand there frozen, listening. Absolutely every single line rings true with me and I feel tears well up in my eyes. 'When you call me baby, I know I'm not the only one.' I was so trusting and totally oblivious to what was going on. I should have known the late nights at work and going out with the lads was a front, but then why would I. I trusted that man with everything I had, every part of me, and he took it all and ran. As the song ends, I feel totally deflated. I dump my coffee in the sink and pull my phone from the dock stopping the playlist in its tracks. Climbing the stairs wearily I head for Steven's bedroom and grab his robe from behind the bathroom door. Pulling it round me I climb into his bed. I send off a text to him.

'I miss you. X'

I put my phone on the bedside table and pull the duvet up around me and cry myself to sleep.

CHAPTER 31

I WAKE IN PITCH black. I can hear someone breathing. Where the hell is that coming from? I sit up and squint my eyes.

"Steven?" I whisper. I hear movement and quicker than I can blink he is by my side. He pulls the duvet back and climbs in beside me wrapping his arms around me and pulling me so close to him he could wear me.

"I missed you too baby. I'm so sorry."

I reach up and touch his face. It is stubbly and wet with tears. "Please don't cry Steven, you have nothing to be sorry for."

We lie in silence. Steven kisses my hair and moves down to my face, round to my lips and the spark that hits me is magic. We kiss passionately, our mouths moving in time with each other. I am so overjoyed to be back in his arms again knowing that this is what love should feel like. His hands skim over my body over my clothes and he pulls me to sit up. He takes my clothes off piece-by-piece and then undresses himself. Our warm naked bodies touching every inch of each other

He holds his face close to mine. "I will never let you go again Gina." His voice is barely a whisper; his hot breath sends shivers up my spine. "Never, not even if you beg me. You are mine and I will love you and only you till the day I die."

He moves me on to my back and kisses me slow and deep, all the while I feel him stiffen against my leg. I am desperate to feel him inside me again. I raise my hands up and hold on to his broad toned shoulders. I can feel the ripple of his muscles as he raises himself up over me. Ever so slowly he eases himself into me and I immediately feel myself moulding to him, opening up for him, stretching, like we were meant to be. Steven moves back onto his knees slightly and with his hands behind my back pulls me up so that I am sitting in his lap. The change in position has him hitting that sweet spot deep inside me. My body moves almost involuntarily as I ride him slowly. I can't get close enough to him. I want to climb inside and possess every molecule of him.

We get into a rhythm with each other. He flexes his hips ever so slightly each time I come down on him and each time my already swollen clit is rubbed a little more. It is getting increasingly hard for me to hold my orgasm back and when he takes my hard nipple in his mouth and nips it lightly, I am done for. I feel the pulses rising through my entire body and the orgasmic glow spread over my cheeks. I am not nearly finished with mine when Steven lets go, forcing his fingers into my hair and squeezing tight as he comes shouting my name over and over again. My muscles are clenching so hard that it feels as if my body is trying to suck him in. The shudders wracking my body are more than just a sexual release; they are a release of everything that came before this. Everything that tainted my very existence and with it goes my memories of Aiden. Even the good ones. The bad far outweigh them and I realise now that I never ever had a connection with him like I do with Steven.

As both of us come down from our high, he tilts my head up towards him and I can see him in the very early dawn light. He looks utterly shattered and I am about to apologise for being the cause of it when he puts his finger on my lips.

"Don't you ever apologise for being in love, do

you hear me? You have done nothing to apologise for."

"Back atcha pal," I say with a tiny half smile.

"I'm so in love with you Gina, I have loved you since the moment I saw you. You have a beautiful soul you know. Wouldn't mind some of that for myself." We snuggle down together; my back against his front, and Steven pulls the duvet over us.

"Good night my beautiful girl."

"Good night handsome." I whisper and at that he pulls me in closer and I feel him smile into my hair. He has a beautiful soul; he just hasn't found it yet. I intend to fix that. As I prepare to embark on this new chapter of my life, I know it won't be easy. Far from it. Steven has a lot of emotional baggage he needs to offload and I have picked up some new bags on the carousel that has been the last week.

As Steven's breathing evens out and I feel his body physically relax, I close my eyes and picture that scared little boy who only wanted a mother to love him, just someone he could call his own. He has a lot of demons he has to expel and I know this is going to be a difficult road for both of us, but I believe in my heart that we will make it, together.

A PAGE FROM THE DIARY OF A PSYCHO

SO YOU GOT ME the jail again you fucking wee bastard. You and that fucking cow Cheryl. Aye we'll see who has the last laugh you wee fucker. I should have done you in too. Ruined ma life ya wee scumbag all because your maw couldn't keep her knickers on. Aye I'll be biding ma time. You wait, I'll fucking get you. I know where tae find you and I'll be oot here soon enough. I'll just play good wee soldier and then I'm coming for you. You'll no see me, but I'll see you. You think what I did to that dirty wee whore was bad wait till I get my hands on your wee bit of stuff. You'll regret the day you ever fucked wi me son, when I'm done wi her you'll no want to look at her again. She'll never see it coming and if I get the chance, I'll make you watch. Oh aye that's what I'll do, I'll make you watch every last thing I dae tae her. She'll be less use than a dirty whore when I'm through. Should a kept your filthy mouth shut son, just like I always told you, just like you did about the other stuff. You'll no tell anybody about that, I know you won't. Wouldn't that look nice on your CV? The papers would have a field day wi that wouldn't they. You wouldn't be the golden boy then. You'd be a disgrace for letting that get done to you in the first place. Aye I canny wait for ma freedom this time, watch yer back boy, I'm going to fuck you up even more than you fucked me up.

Thanks for reading

Gina and Steven will return

Read on for a look at the first few
chapters of Saviour of the Soul,
Book 2 in the Soul Series

Keep up to date with news and
upcoming book releases by visiting:
www.clstewart.co.uk

Sign up for exclusive content and
offers

SAVIOUR OF THE SOUL

PROLOGUE

THE YELLOWING PAINTED BRICK walls of the prison cell comfort him. Prison is basically his home. Really who wouldn't like it? Three meals a day, TV in his cell and, most of the time, a decent cell mate.

He likes routine. Routine helps him with his plans. Okay getting jailed again wasn't part of the plan. He was stupid to think Cheryl wouldn't do something when she found out he had been released. He hadn't counted on her getting friendly with Steven though. Why would he? She hated Steven almost as much as he did.

Best to bide his time and play nice. There's always somebody willing to do things on the outside for the right price and when he eventually gets out, he'll make them pay. All of them, and they won't know what's hit them.

CHAPTER 1

WHENEVER I THINK OF Christmas I am reminded of my childhood when the festive season started as soon as it hit the first of December. Mum would pester dad to get the tree and decorations down from the attic so that we could festoon the house. We always started with the lights. Testing them to make sure they still worked. In the days before LED lights if one bulb was out the whole string didn't work. Many a first of December was spent pulling and replacing every bulb to find out which one had blown. Inevitably it would always be the last one, no matter which end you started at.

Our house always ended up looking like a scene from Elf. Even when she was finished, she wasn't really finished. Every time she would go shopping or come home from work, she would have '*just one more thing*' to add to Santa's Grotto. Dad eventually gave up, just smiled and let her get on with it.

My childhood Christmases were very happy. My childhood was very happy full stop, so you can imagine my shock at Steven's reaction when I mentioned putting up a Christmas tree in his apartment earlier this morning.

***

"Do you have a tree and decorations? This place needs some festivity. It's only a week till Christmas."

"I don't do Christmas." Steven declared with his back to me reading some papers.

"You don't do Christmas?"

"No.".

"Who on earth doesn't do Christmas? It's such a fun time of the year."

He shook his head and I could see his fists clench. "For fuck sake Gina leave it."

"I don't think there was any call for that Steven. I was only asking."

He turned to look at me, his expression solemn and angry. "Think about it Gina. I mean really think about what you are saying here before you go any further."

Light bulb.

"Tell me Gina, would you celebrate Christmas if every single one you had as a child was only another day? If every Christmas you saw kids out on their new bikes or in their new clothes. If so many fucking Christmas dinners were a tin of beans or whatever you could find that wasn't out of date." He closed his eyes and shook his head. "If every fucking day you lived in... Oh forget it Gina."

"I'm sorry Steven, I didn't think."

"No that's the problem when you've never had to deal with that sort of thing Gina. You think everyone lived in the same wee bubble you did." He lifted his papers and walked to the kitchen door.

"Where are you going? I said I was sorry."

"I have work to do." And with that he walked away leaving me sitting alone in the kitchen. God that was harsh. I heard him go upstairs and then a door slammed. Thank God, I had a horrible feeling he was going to walk out.

***

It's a little after three in the afternoon and the natural light is already fading. I haven't seen Steven since he went up to his office about four hours ago. I grab my phone and take the stairs as quietly as I can. I head into his walk-in wardrobe and gather up the

Sexy Santa outfit he gave me. I really hope he sees the funny side of this and I don't look like a complete fool. I forego the boots this time, they make too much noise, and after plugging my iPhone into the dock in the bedroom I select the Christmas playlist. If this doesn't get me back in the good books, I don't know what will.

As the first strains of *'Santa Baby'* fill the speakers I tentatively open the office door. Steven's desk sits to the left of it facing the window. Hiding behind the door I stick my left leg out so that he can see it in all its candy cane glory. I put my hands down to my ankle and pull them up slowly. As the singing starts, I step into the room and see that Steven keeps his head down pretending he doesn't see me. I start my seductive little routine. I probably look ridiculous, but I really don't care. Standing with my back to him I gyrate my hips and stick out my bum and when I catch a glimpse of the now darkened window pane in front of me, I see that he is looking at me. And he is smiling. '*Yes! Victory'*.

I make my way over to him, grab the arms of the chair and pull it far enough away from the desk so that I can straddle his lap.

The song finishes and Frank Sinatra comes crooning through the speakers. He looks into my eyes and smiles.

"What are you doing Gina?"

"Oh nothing."

"Does that feel like nothing?" He says as he pulls me closer to him, I can feel his erection through his jeans.

"Mmmm, absolutely not."

He puts his hands behind my head and pulls my lips to his. Our kiss is slow and sweet and seems to last forever. "I'm sorry Gina." Steven whispers against my lips as I lean back to look at him.

"Forget about it, I have. I get it Steven. I'm an idiot. I have this sort of malfunction; you know that brain to mouth thing. Sorry honey but it's just another one of those things you're going to have to love me for." I cock my head to the side and give him a little smile and a flutter of my eyelids. He throws his head back and laughs, a real hearty laugh that vibrates through me. His hands run down my back over the velour of the dress and come to rest on my backside.

"Gina, I am loving every little thing I am finding out about you." He looks down and gives a little shake of his head. "This isn't going to be easy is it?" He looks up at me and I can see the torment behind his eyes.

"No it's not but you know something, look at what we've been through already. I have a feeling we'll be fine." I try my best to reassure him, but my own doubts start to creep in. When you have had your world pulled from under you it is hard to believe in anything

Steven kisses the top of my arm. "Want to go out for dinner?"

His ability to U-turn a subject frustrates me at times but right now it's a welcome relief. As much as we need to talk about things that have gone on in our own lives, what happened to me is still raw, the wounds still too fresh.

"Sounds good to me. Shall we toss for it?"

"That sounds like heaven to me babe, but we might never make it to dinner if I let you do that." He throws me a sexy wink laughing at his own joke.

I swat him on the chest. "Oh you insatiable beast."

As I stand up and turn away from him, he smacks my bum. "What can I do when you are dressed like that? I'm at your mercy woman."

"Right since your mind is firmly in the gutter, I'm choosing the cuisine. We'll do Italian tonight. I'm off to get dressed."

"You could go like that, I wouldn't mind."

I smile and pick up a cushion from the sofa in front of the window. "Beast." I laugh as I throw it at him. Then I bolt like a bat out of hell before he catches up with me.

CHAPTER 2

"GINA, GERRY IS HERE. Are you ready?" He shouts up the stairs.

Gerry has been summoned to pick us up and the Bentley is sitting at the kerb outside.

I am still trying to get ready. Steven had the car here within fifteen minutes of me suggesting an Italian for dinner.

I open the bedroom door and shout back. "Good God man do you realise how long it takes a lady to get ready. I still have to get dressed."

"Hurry up darling time is money." I can hear the smile in his voice.

I choose a pair of plain black trousers and an off-white sleeveless shell top and black jacket. It looks smart enough for dinner but not too dressed up. Steven took me shopping a few days ago and I now have a well-stocked wardrobe in one of his spare rooms. I settle on a pair of silver sparkly sandals and, with a quick check of my appearance in the mirror on the landing, I head downstairs.

Steven is standing next to the piano with his back to me fiddling on his phone and turns when he hears me. "Very nice," he says and moves towards me as I stand on the second last step. He lifts me in his arms and kisses me as I slide down him to stand on the floor.

"Not so bad yourself handsome."

He looks casually yummy in his silvery grey dress trousers and white shirt with the sleeves rolled to slightly below the elbows. God his forearms should be illegal.

"Let's go before I tell Gerry to go and get us a take away instead." He winks at me and pulls me towards the door.

"Okay Mr Insatiable. Watch it…you may wear me out."

"That's my plan babe," he laughs.

Gerry is waiting outside and opens the door as soon as he sees us.

"Evening folks," he says and nods. "Looking lovely Gina as always."

"Thanks Gerry, as do you." I flash him a smile and look at Steven who is giving Gerry the evil eye.

"Sorry sir, you look good too," says Gerry with a smile. Ooh he's brave.

"You're a funny man Gerry. It's a good thing I like you." They both shake hands and I see the affection Steven has for Gerry in the look he gives the man. It's nice to see.

I get into the back of the car and Steven joins me. He places his hand on my thigh as Gerry closes the door. It's nice, but I am still very wary of every little thing that feels too good to be true.

A little over a week ago I got the shock of my life when I found out that my dead husband had been having an affair which had produced a child. And in a seriously messed up twist of fate I ended up having to help the girl deliver the baby after she ambushed me in my own home. It is constantly in the back of my mind that the one person I thought was the love of my life betrayed me. He was the one person I thought would always protect me.

I thought we were happy. It turns out I was the stupid sap who wanted to believe that there was good in everyone. Boy, how wrong was I? It made me realise that nothing in this life is certain or sure, that there are always going to be obstacles to overcome.

It is much harder to be happy than it is to be

miserable. Being miserable is easy you only need to shut yourself down. I know, I did it. Making yourself happy, no scratch that, allowing yourself to be happy takes hard work, time and plenty of soul searching. It also needs trust. That's what I know I am going to have the most trouble with. I know not everyone is the same; I know Steven is nothing like Aiden. In the four weeks or so I have known him he has managed to capture my heart. He has made me feel alive again and has done nothing but make me feel loved and safe. He has promised me he will never let me down.

I want so badly to believe him. I know I believe him on some level, but it will take time to get over what has happened. I can only hope his will is strong enough to hang around.

As the car pulls to a stop, I notice we are in a little side street off High Street in the city centre. This does not look like the sort of place a millionaire businessman takes his girlfriend to dinner. Yes, girlfriend, I have finally accepted that accolade, much to my best friend Charlie's relief.

Steven leans in to me and kisses my hair. "We're here babe. You hungry?"

"Yes, but where is here?"

"Ah, it's a surprise."

"Yay I just love surprises." Sarcasm drips from my voice and he smiles at me cheekily as we exit the car.

"I'll call you if I need you Gerry. Are you okay to be on standby tonight?"

"Sure am mate, on my lonesome tonight."

"Great, I'll let you know what's happening." He closes the door and gives the top of the car a slap.

As Gerry drives off, we walk towards the small shop front. It blends in with the other buildings and you would think it was a greasy spoon cafe. There is a queue outside, but Steven walks past them all and through the red door. We get some annoyed looks as we enter the building. The smell of garlic and herbs hits my nose and instantly makes my mouth water.

The interior of the restaurant is small and very cosy. There are six tables covered with white tablecloths and simple dark wood chairs. It is all very minimalistic but my God the food smells amazing.

As we stand in the doorway a young waitress comes over to us and hugs Steven. "Hi there honey, how are you?"

"Hi Rosa, I'm good. This is my girlfriend Gina." He introduces me and I immediately feel goose bumps form on my skin. His girlfriend. It sounds so nice coming out of his mouth.

Rosa holds out her hand. "Pleased to meet you Gina. Nice Italian name by the way."

"Nice to meet you too and I wish I could say it

was Italian. It's actually short for Georgina. I think it's actually Dutch."

"Well it's Italian tonight," she laughs and shakes my hand.

"Is he in tonight Rosa?" Steven asks.

"Yes I'll go and tell him you're here. Take a seat."

We sit at the only empty table and Rosa disappears into the back.

"This place is nice, it's intimate isn't it," I say as I look around.

"Yes, it is. The food is amazing."

"I take it you come here a lot since the waitress knows you so well. Or do you own this place too?" I giggle but then I notice the smile on Steven's face.

"Oh for goodness sake do you own the whole of Glasgow?"

He laughs. I shake my head and pour a glass of water from the jug on the table.

"Not the whole city but I do have my fingers in a lot of pies."

I almost choke on my drink.

"Oh Gina get your mind out the gutter." He chastises me with a wicked grin on his face.

I am still trying to deal with my flushed cheeks when a booming Italian voice with a hint of a Scottish accent comes from behind me. "Steven my boy. Looking good son."

Steven stands up and shakes the large hand of the man standing beside our table. He looks like he could be in his late sixties.

"Ricco, looking good yourself."

"Ah you wee charmer. And who is this beautiful girl you've brought with you?"

"This is my girlfriend Gina."

"Ah…bellissima. Pleased to meet you Gina." He kisses the back of my hand. He is tall with silvery grey hair and I can tell he was a handsome man in his younger years.

"Pleased to meet you too Ricco. This is a cosy little place you have here."

"Thanks my dear but you can thank your good man here for the fact that it is still here at all. Right I'll get Rosa to get you drinks and a menu." He pats Steven on the back. "It's good to see you son."

"So what happened with this place then?" I ask as we wait for Rosa to come back.

"I went to University with Ricco's grandson. Dario was one of my best friends at Uni. Rosa is Dario's wee sister. Ricco's daughter died when the children were very young. Her husband committed suicide and she eventually drank herself to death. Ricco and his wife basically brought the kids up."

"What happened to Dario?" I ask.

"When he was twenty-three, he was diagnosed

with testicular cancer but by the time he had gone to see a doctor it was too late for them to help. His body was riddled with it. He passed away two years ago. Ricco went into a downward spiral and got into serious debt. The restaurant was going to be repossessed and I couldn't bear to see them suffer anymore. I offered to buy the place for them and sell it back when they were back on their feet."

"So it's not actually yours then, you're only babysitting it."

"Well, no, it is mine. Ricco doesn't want to buy it back. He says the minute I offered to buy the place he felt ten years younger. I think he feels he's too old to handle the stress. We came to a compromise. I would buy it and be a silent owner and he would run the place without all the stress of being responsible for the bills."

"You're a good guy Steven you know that? So what's the food like?" The smell of the cooking coming from the kitchen is making my stomach growl.

"Oh the food is amazing. Ricco is a fantastic chef. He's from Sardinia originally and, like a lot of Italians, he was taught to cook by his family. The food is just so..." He pauses for a second and looks up slightly to his left as if he's trying to remember something.

I burst out laughing and hit such a fit of the giggles that I can't stop until the tears are streaming down my face.

Steven looks at me with amused bewilderment. "Are you okay Gina? What's so funny?"

"Oh God Steven I am so sorry. You did Joey's 'Smell the Fart Acting'."

His puzzled expression stops my giggles dead.

"Please tell me you have watched Friends? Oh God I wish Charlie was here. We used to watch it constantly when we were at Uni. We'd do all-nighters and binge watch them. Aiden..." I stop talking. Even the mention of that bastard's name makes me want to throw up.

"Fuck it," I say under my breath and instantly my happy, bubbly feeling is gone.

"Friends was actually one of my favourites, but I only watched it because more often than not at least one of the girls had a good nipple shot. Jennifer Aniston was my favourite," he says with a huge smile. Expert of the U-turn.

I smile back. "Beast."

***

The food certainly outdid Steven's description. I now understand why this place is busy with a queue like an execution out the door. I sit back in my chair and place my hands on the table.

"Oh God Steven that was hands down the best Italian meal I have ever had and I've been to Italy."

"I told you he was good, didn't I?" He reaches across the table and takes both of my hands in his. "It's nice to see you smiling gorgeous." He runs his thumbs over my knuckles. "How do you fancy coming with me to find a Christmas tree for the house?"

"Really?"

"Yes really. I am so sorry about earlier."

He gives me a little half smile.

"I'm going to make it up to you. We can get the tree tonight and we can go and get decorations for it tomorrow."

"Oh no we don't just decorate the tree. I'm going to make your house look like ten North Poles in one so when Santa visits, he'll think he's come home." I can't hide my excitement; I'm like a bloody child.

38307647R00197

Printed in Great Britain
by Amazon